# "Did you really think I would allow you to take advantage of me?"

Guy demanded, delivering the rebuke in a fierce, teasing voice.

He was so close she could see the tiny aquamarine flecks in his dazzling gray eyes...so close they seemed to share the same breath, the same air.

"Take advantage of you!" Kate gasped, knowing she was pinned so securely he could do anything he liked with her. "Let me go...let me go!" she exclaimed, fighting to stop her gaze lingering on his mouth. But he had captured her wrists in one hand, while his other posed a delicious threat as it hovered over her, reducing her to writhing on the ground, to his obvious entertainment.

"How can I let you go?" he said—as if there might have been the slightest chance he would. "Wildcats must be tamed."

# Susan Stephens

## THE FRENCH COUNT'S MISTRESS

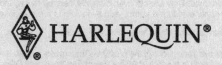

# HARLEQUIN®

TORONTO • NEW YORK • LONDON
AMSTERDAM • PARIS • SYDNEY • HAMBURG
STOCKHOLM • ATHENS • TOKYO • MILAN • MADRID
PRAGUE • WARSAW • BUDAPEST • AUCKLAND

ISBN 0-373-12342-6

THE FRENCH COUNT'S MISTRESS

First North American Publication 2003.

Copyright © 2003 by Susan Stephens.

Visit us at www.eHarlequin.com

**Printed in U.S.A.**

# CHAPTER ONE

'BUT, *mademoiselle*… Monsieur le Comte is in a meeting. He is not receiving anyone.'

'He will see me,' Kate Foster said confidently, sweeping past the liveried servant into a vast room that seemed little changed over the years.

But she had changed, Kate thought in the split second between taking in her surroundings and identifying her quarry. She was not intimidated, as she had been as a child, maybe because success allowed her to weigh material possessions on a very different set of scales. A group of men seated around an oval table in the centre of the room turned to stare as she approached, then they got to their feet, but only one held her interest.

'Kate?' he exclaimed softly.

The commanding voice connected with something so deep she had to fight to keep her eye-line steady. She had forgotten how tall he was…how striking… Guy de Villeneuve wasn't just handsome; he seemed to have been formed from exclusive constituents. His tanned skin appeared more luminous, his ebony hair lusher, his lashes longer, his sable brows more expressive and his lips—she looked away quickly, conscious that she too was being appraised, and those piercing steel-grey eyes were a vivid reminder of what awaited anyone foolish enough to be swept away by the Count de Villeneuve's dazzling good looks. No, Kate reminded herself, the Count's strongest suit had always been his iron will and fierce intelligence, gifts he cloaked behind the deceptive guise of inborn elegance, and… Her cheeks flamed when she recognised another, more elusive quality to be smouldering sensuality.

5

Pretending interest in several seascapes hanging on the wall, she allowed her gaze to diffuse and seek multiple targets rather than the one devastating individual waiting across the room. Even if courtesy had forced him to accept her intrusion, Kate knew that very different emotions would be brewing behind his hawkish stare.

'Count Guy de Villeneuve,' she said as she reached him, keeping the greeting intentionally cool.

His sardonic query at the formal style of address showed briefly in his eyes, but as far as Kate was concerned it was ten years since they had last met and this was not a social visit. She had followed Guy de Villeneuve's career closely enough to know that charm and beauty were common currency in his world. Anyone foolish enough to imagine that feminine wiles could possibly influence him where business was concerned would soon discover their mistake. She could almost see the cogs flying round in his mind. Reading her mood had always been easy for him, she remembered, watching his steel-grey eyes narrow with conjecture. Now she was back in a familiar game—one in which he was used to taking the lead. A game where provoking the short-fused, Titian-haired visitor to his family's vast estate had been an annual amusement for the young Count. But ten years had intervened since their last spat. Ten years in which she had built up and lost one career and was currently riding the crest of another. Ten years in which she had learned to deal with men like—

'So, Kate,' he said, cutting into her thoughts. 'It's been a long time. How can I help you?'

Halting a safe distance away, Kate flicked back her glossy tumble of hair, thankful that she knew the rules of his game now. But today she was seeking a very different outcome from Guy, Count de Villeneuve. And she needed to move things along fast.

'Kate?'

The warmth had spilt from his eyes, leaving something

hard to pin down but troubling, and for a split second she wondered if she had made a mistake coming to him direct. The deep, lightly accented voice was seductive and disarming and it was hard to ignore the fact that ten years had only honed his lean athletic frame into an even higher state of perfection. Dragging her gaze away, Kate inclined her head just a little to acknowledge the slight dip of his head. 'I apologise for the intrusion, Monsieur le Comte, but I really must speak to you.'

'About what, exactly?'

He was a good head taller than the men around him, with a face that might have graced a movie screen had the expression in his eyes been more calculated to disarm, Kate thought, watching as he made a gesture to suggest that his colleagues should be seated. Lifting her chin, she took a few steps towards him. 'It's a matter I should like to discuss with you in private.'

'As you can see, I am in a meeting. My secretary—'

'This won't wait.' She was pleased to hear her voice so steady as she drew herself up to confront him. But it was impossible not to notice the speculation behind his faintly amused gaze and she was relieved when he turned away briefly to study some documents on the table in front of him.

'An appointment would have made everything possible,' he said evenly, but when he glanced up a flash of something hot in his eyes belied the reasonable tone of voice.

The implied challenge only fanned Kate's determination and the characteristic glow in her emerald eyes dwindled then froze into shards of green ice. 'I telephoned your secretary before I left England, asking for an appointment, but she said your diary was full for the rest of this month.'

The Count brought his head up slowly to confront her. 'Did you leave your name, *mademoiselle*?' His stress on the last word was intentional—calculated to provoke. It did its job.

'Yes, of course,' Kate retorted in a clipped tone that suggested he should know her better than to imagine she was so inept. But how could he know anything about her? she realised with a jolt, stopping short of slipping into the combative argot of her youth. Guy de Villeneuve only knew the child she had been and not the woman she had become. 'I asked your secretary most specifically to inform you that Kate Foster had called.' She was pleased to hear the change in her voice—and to see a shadow briefly darken the Count's face as he realised that a member of his staff was to blame for the oversight. But she also knew he was far too subtle to make his displeasure public.

'Well, Kate Foster,' he said, enunciating each syllable with sardonic precision. 'Until I know what it is you want to talk to me about, I can hardly be expected to ask these gentlemen to leave.'

Kate confined herself to a raised brow as their eyes clashed, but then her gaze was drawn to a muscle flexing in his jaw—a jaw that was already shaded with stubble so early in the day. Her eyes flickered up to his lips and bounced away again fast—but not before she had seen the knowing smile tugging remorselessly at the corners of his mouth.

It both troubled and excited her to know he hadn't lost the art of reading her responses. Out of the corner of her eye she could see the other men beginning to relax. The confrontation promised some light relief for them. She blanked them out. 'I am here to discuss La Petite Maison.'

The Count responded to the hard edge in her voice with a stare of almost hypnotic intensity before swinging around to address his colleagues. 'Gentlemen, forgive me. We will reconvene this meeting tomorrow morning at nine.'

Round one to her, Kate thought, relaxing minutely. She waited in silence until the room cleared, lifting her chin in resolute defiance as the men walked past her, gazing with naked interest at the woman who presumed to interrupt the schedule of the Count de Villeneuve.

'Won't you sit down?' the Count invited as the door finally closed on the last of them.

Kate glanced at the two easy chairs facing each other across a fireplace carved from a single block of Carrara marble and then back again to the confident individual standing in front of her. The Count's suggestion would immediately put her at the receiving end of his legendary hospitality rather than on the opposing side of what might well turn into a legal dispute between them. 'I prefer to stand, if you don't mind.'

'As you wish.'

As if sensing her unease, the Count remained where he was...too far away to touch, but close enough for her to detect the scent of warm clean man overlaid with the aroma of citrus fruits and spice.

'Kate, *se passe*? Have you forgotten me?'

Kate's face flared red as she met his amused gaze. How could she forget? Instinctively her gaze slipped to his lips.

'Is it all coming back to you now?' he murmured with what she suspected was more than a hint of satisfaction.

The heat teasing her senses was proof enough...but that same delicious sensation served as a warning too. 'I haven't come here to reminisce,' she said firmly. 'My only concern is for the present—'

'Mine, too,' he assured her smoothly. Turning on his heel, he strode away from her across the peach-veined marble floor to where an intricately inlaid cherry wood desk stood in front of a tall arched window. 'Won't you come and sit down?' he invited, holding out a chair opposite to his own comfortably padded leather swivel seat.

His gaze was like a silken lasso drawing her across the room, Kate thought, fighting the urge to move.

'Come,' he urged gently, as if dealing with a highly bred

mare. 'Come and tell me what's on your mind, Kate. Whatever your problem, I'm sure I can find a solution for you.'

His containment was driving her crazy, she realised, consciously steadying her breathing. His inflexible control had always brought out the worst in her. But, even as she told herself that she had changed beyond recognition in the years since they had last met, she found herself thrusting one hand on to the swell of her hip and speaking to him in the same furious tone she had once adopted as a self-willed teenager.

'Talking won't solve this problem, I'm afraid.'

'May I ask what *would* satisfy you?' he enquired, the gleam in his eyes betraying not only his recognition, but his enjoyment of her lapse.

The answer that sprang unbidden into Kate's mind made her eyes widen with alarm. Guy de Villeneuve was in his late thirties and occupied the front cover of *Time* magazine with almost monotonous regularity. Kate, for all her commercial success, was just brushing twenty-six and had a life devoted to work, where there was no time for romance, let alone the type of relationship her over-active imagination had just conjured up.

'Now you're here it won't hurt you to relax,' he continued reasonably. 'Can you come away from the door? I don't bite.'

It was impossible to read his face…but it had been more than ten years, Kate reminded herself. She was out of practice. But if he thought he could make her nervous…make her forget the reason for her visit… She started walking towards him with her head held high and her dancer's carriage almost concealing the slight limp that was the legacy of the accident that had almost killed her.

'It would be a start if you could explain why La Petite Maison has been so badly neglected,' she agreed frostily.

Now it was the Count's turn to grow still as he watched

her progress towards him. 'Ah, that,' he murmured distractedly.

'Yes, that,' Kate agreed. 'Well?' she pressed. 'How *do* you explain it? I have been paying money into the Villeneuve estate office for almost six months now. Money I imagined would more than cover any necessary maintenance on the cottage until I was in a position to come over here and take charge for myself.'

'*Oh, par pitie, Kate!*' His elegant gesture silenced her. 'It was understood by all the tenants that as soon as I had restored the estate to its original purpose the holiday cottages would have to go.'

'Well, I wasn't informed,' Kate said as she settled into the chair he was holding out for her. 'Under the circumstances, don't you think your behaviour has been a little high-handed?'

As he took the seat facing her the Count's powerful shoulders lifted in a shrug. 'I apologise for the oversight. When Madame Broadbent passed on I received no word regarding her intentions for La Petite Maison. I had no reason to believe that she left the cottage to you. Without the benefit of formal communication I drew the only assumption possible—'

'Which was?' Kate cut in. What was wrong with her pulse? She always remained calm when difficulties in business cropped up—that was her strength, she reminded herself forcefully. And La Petite Maison certainly represented a difficulty, if only because she had allowed her many other interests to take precedence.

The letters from Aunt Alice's solicitor had coincided with the closure of a deal that would see her Internet travel service open at several sites in Japan…she had barely scanned the documents from France.

'I concluded that Madame Broadbent's heirs merely wished to keep the cottage in good repair— Please, let me finish,' the Count insisted quietly when Kate's agitation threatened to become vocal. 'As that was not in line with my own plans, I instructed my estate manager to return all monies paid. On top of that there would have been a generous capital payment in line with the sums I have released to regain full title to all the other properties. Some banking hiccup—'

'You can stop right there,' Kate insisted, pushing a slender hand through her barely contained hair and dragging the rest of it down from the clip in the process. 'I don't want your money, but I do want everything I paid into the Villeneuve estate office to be spent on the cottage.'

'I can't do that—'

'Can't, or won't?' she demanded tensely.

The Count missed a beat, but his eyes had grown dangerously warm as he leaned over the desk to gaze at her. 'Ah, Kate,' he drawled. 'You always were too impetuous—'

'That isn't an answer,' she warned, trying not to notice the attractive way his eyes crinkled at the corners and the dense sweep of ebony lashes that framed the molten steel gaze. His scrutiny was bad enough when she wanted to talk business, but the effect it was having on her senses was nothing short of catastrophic. 'If you refuse to do anything about the cottage,' she said, 'just return the money and I'll sort it out myself.'

'All right,' he agreed, surprising her with his sudden capitulation. 'I'll have all the money repaid into your bank account tomorrow morning.' But, just as Kate felt some of her tension seep away, he added starkly, 'But the cottage reverts to me. You will accept my offer.'

'Blackmail?' she said as she got to her feet.

The Count's fist slammed down on his desk. *'T'exagere!'* Gathering himself quickly, he stood up, his dark, brooding expression an unmistakable mark of reproof. 'I prefer to call it an amicable arrangement,' he said in a low voice.

'It's a very one-sided arrangement,' Kate observed, with

remarkable composure considering she was confronting a gaze grown more dangerous than she could ever remember, 'and hardly amicable since I don't want any part of it.'

'Perhaps when you hear what I have to say you might change your mind.'

Kate's heart was thundering out of control, but still she managed evenly, 'I doubt it.'

'So you won't even listen to my offer?'

As he stood towering over her, waiting for her reply, Kate drew herself up, but even when she was at full stretch he was still a good head taller...and there was a glint in his eyes that suggested he was actually entertained by her stand. Now she *was* mad. 'Don't patronise me, Guy. I'm a grown woman with my own business to run.'

'And I thought you'd forgotten how to say my name,' he growled softly.

His voice was as dark and deliciously beguiling as bitter chocolate, Kate realised as she struggled to keep her mind focused on the purpose of her visit.

Perhaps it was the timbre of his speech, or maybe the pitch, but something primitive was strumming her senses with a persistent and unmistakable beat. And if past experience had left her with the misleading notion that she was immune to machismo, Guy, Count de Villeneuve had just proved her wrong. And he knew it, she realised as their glances clashed.

'Don't change the subject,' Kate warned, rallying fast. 'You know what I'm here for and it isn't a trip down memory lane.'

In a few electric moments their eyes met and held. Then, raising his eyebrows the merest fraction, he said, 'I think we should both calmly put our cards on the table.'

'I won't change my mind.'

'As you please, Kate,' the Count said as he dropped on to his chair. 'But whatever you've got to say, make it brief. I've got a great many things to do.' He tossed her a look

that was suddenly a good deal less tolerant, and she noticed
how one of his hands seemed to want to mash the end of
a bone-handled paperknife. The unconscious gesture was
so much at odds with his strong watchful face that Kate
was forced to wonder if she was as disturbing to him as he
was to her. One thing was clear: he would soon lose pa-
tience with her again. It seemed that even Guy de
Villeneuve's fabled courtesy had its limitations—

'Well?' he pressed. 'Do you intend to join me any time
soon? Or would you prefer just to stand there and stare?'

The roughness in his voice was even more seductive than
the charm, Kate realised as she moved to perch on the very
edge of the chair. Smoothing her delicate aquamarine-tinted
muslin skirt around her bare tanned legs, she watched him
select a folder from the neat pile in front of him. But her
gaze, like her thoughts, soon began to wander.

Ten years before she had been a gawky teenager with a
helpless crush on a French aristocrat. Today she sat before
the same man, close enough to see the silver wings that
time had laced through his thick, wavy black hair—sat before him as a successful woman in her own right, thanks
to the runaway success of her Internet travel business. But
how did that help when her heart was beating so fast she
could hardly breathe? Awe and desire had once consumed
her adolescent dreams. It was a real shock to discover that
the Count could still provoke those same complex feelings—only now it was worse, far worse, she acknowledged.
Now she wasn't an innocent young girl, but a successful
working woman with all the appetites that went with the
dynamic territory she inhabited. And there had been no
time to assuage those appetites during the crazy rollercoaster ride to the top—or any real temptation before this
moment, she realised as she drank in the athletic figure
beneath the impeccably cut suit.

'Ready, Kate?'

She snapped back to attention instantly, irritated by the

lapse. She had come to level a complaint against this man, not sum up his potential as a lover! As her fingers strayed to check the fastenings on her casual blouse, she cursed the fact that she hadn't thought to change into one of her Armani suits. Infuriated by the state of the cottage she had reacted without thinking, jumping into her rented Jeep to beard the lion in his den. But an outfit that had been perfectly acceptable in the balmy French countryside had suddenly become an embarrassment to her when she was locked in confrontation with a man like Guy de Villeneuve. It was far too revealing, for one thing, and had obviously sent out the wrong signals. The Count's responses so far suggested that he found her capricious and provocative, rather than lucid and determined.

Kate's mind blanked as a pair of perceptive grey eyes levelled a gaze of remorseless enquiry upon her face and a very seductive mouth began to curve in the suspicion of a smile. Then with mercurial speed his glance switched to her naked shoulders and began drifting over the sun-kissed flesh to where a swell of ivory showed with each breath she took. And the flimsy skirt was practically transparent, she remembered, hastily wrapping it around her legs.

The low voice reached her across the desk even though his attention appeared to have returned to the documents in front of him. 'Careful...it would be a shame to crush such a lovely skirt.' The compliment might have sounded innocent enough to anyone who didn't know the Count, but Kate remembered him well enough to realise that his senses were so keenly tuned he missed nothing—nothing at all. And that was a real concern as she had just eased position in response to a rogue shaft of sensation.

*'C'est très jolie,'* he murmured before glancing up. 'Very you.'

The comment puzzled Kate for a moment. Then she realised that, just as she had her own childhood memories, the Count would always think of her as the little girl who visited his family estate to holiday at her aunt's cottage. The casual two-piece she was wearing now was very similar in style to the clothes Aunt Alice used to have waiting for her, outfits laid out neatly on the high French bed that had been Kate's for the duration of her stay. The brightly coloured garments have given her such pleasure—such escape from her rigid existence at home. It had always felt as if she was stepping into a different world when she put them on, as if she could be someone else altogether—at least for the summer. She hadn't even made the connection when she had purchased the traditional blouse and skirt at the open-air market on her first day back in France. She realised now that it had been a major part of the fantasy she had hoped to recreate—the fantasy the compelling individual in front of her seemed intent on demolishing.

'I haven't got all day, Kate,' he prompted.

Yes, she thought irritably. The indulgent note in his voice was unmistakable. He did think of her as that little girl. She had brought it upon herself. All those years of carving a niche for herself in one of the most competitive business arenas had been erased in a moment by market stall clothes.

'Kate?' His voice had grown sharper. 'I'm sorry, Kate, but I really must insist—'

His tone of voice left her in no doubt that they had almost passed the point where she had any credibility left. Guy de Villeneuve's switch from sexual predator to time-starved tycoon was effortless and Kate knew she would have to match his mood or capitulate.

'I'm not selling the cottage back to you,' she said at last. 'I'm going to live in it.'

The Count's face betrayed no emotion whatever as he reached for a folder from a pile stacked in front of him.

'Well?' Kate pressed. 'Don't you have anything to say?'

'There are a few things I think I need to explain to you about La Petite Maison,' he said as he slipped some documents from the folder and laid them out on the desk.

'I disagree,' Kate said firmly. 'It all seems pretty clear to me. The cottage used to belong to my aunt, Madame Broadbent. And now it belongs to me.'

'I am aware that the cottage you refer to was included in the estate of Madame Broadbent,' the Count agreed evenly. 'But until today—'

'You had no idea—'

'To whom she had bequeathed it,' he murmured as he scanned the papers. After checking them briefly he pushed them across the desk to her.

'Before I look at these,' Kate said, fixing him with a determined stare, 'I would like to know what has happened to the money I have been paying into your estate office. You can't tell me there isn't a record—' She stopped. Something in his expression warned her that this was not the moment to jump on her high horse.

'I am aware of every payment received for La Petite Maison,' the Count assured her. 'But those transactions show nothing more than a company name.' Picking out a couple more sheets, he passed them over to her.

Kate's stomach contracted. Even Guy de Villeneuve could not be expected to know that Freedom Holidays was her company. But that didn't excuse the state of the cottage. As she felt his gaze resting on her she pretended interest in the invoice... But his sexual aura was lapping around her senses, clouding her mind with erotic images that had nothing to do with the purpose of her visit.

'But if all these payments are in order,' she began huskily, 'how do you explain the neglect at the cottage?' She tossed the invoices back across the desk to avoid looking at him.

'Ancient covenants govern La Petite Maison just the same as they do all the other cottages on the estate. Also it is leasehold. Accordingly, I don't need to explain my actions. The fact that I choose to—'

'You choose to?' Kate flared, even though her logical mind told her he was acting honourably.

*'Certainement,'* he confirmed.

'So, no one has any rights except you?' Her emotional self took another battering as he answered her heated question with just a slight lift of his shoulders.

'Who else did you imagine owned the land on which all the estate cottages stand, Kate?'

'You—' She found herself flailing about mentally, wondering why on earth she hadn't confronted this obvious fact before. Why had she chosen to ignore the reality of Guy de Villeneuve as a neighbour? And now it seemed as landlord too!

'That is correct,' he said, making a bridge of his fingers on which to rest his chin.

She knew he was waiting to see what her response would be now she knew he held all the cards. Well, that look might have weakened other women— 'I have found no record of my aunt ever making a payment for ground rent,' she said, confronting the gaze he was levelling at her with an unwavering stare. 'And I have checked through every one of her documents thoroughly—'

'All except the deeds for the cottage, I presume,' he observed, keeping his eyes trained on her face.

As she watched them darken from silver-grey to steel and then grow blacker still she raced to gather her wits while she still had some left. 'Well, yes,' she admitted. 'I left that to my solicitor. And he said...' Her voice tailed away.

Mr Jones had been at pains to explain that property law pertaining to ancient estates in France could be quite a minefield. He had asked her to make an appointment so that they could have a proper discussion regarding his many concerns. But she had been too busy to meet him—too busy making plans for this, her new venture.

As if scenting victory, the Count had grown very still

like a jungle cat about to pounce. 'It was remiss of your solicitor not to mention—'

'No,' Kate admitted reluctantly. 'I am the one to blame. My solicitor wanted to go through everything with me in detail. I just haven't had time—'

'Ah,' the Count said as if to imply that she might have done better to slow down and prioritise. 'Is there something else?' he added shrewdly.

'Yes,' Kate said, feeling she was on to something. 'You still haven't explained why there are no records of Aunt Alice ever making payment for a lease—'

'Madame Broadbent was never asked for money,' the Count revealed quietly. 'As one of my mother's closest friends it would have been highly inappropriate to exact any form of payment from her.'

'You seemed to have no trouble accepting mine,' Kate said, feeling unaccountably stung by this revelation.

'All your payments will be returned with interest.'

'But I don't want them returned. I want the money spent on the cottage,' she insisted again.

'*C'est impossible,*' he said with finality. 'There will no longer be any independent cottages on my estate.'

'What are you talking about?'

Unfolding his impressive frame, the Count got to his feet. 'You will find my offer more than generous,' he said in a voice that suggested their meeting was over. 'I can assure you that everyone else has been more than satisfied—'

'Oh, really?'

'*Oui, vraiment.*' His voice was clipped and dry, but abruptly his steely gaze softened. 'Come on, Katie,' he urged. 'What do you need a second home in France for if you are so busy—?'

'My name is Kate!' Kate flared, horrified to hear the break in her voice.

'Kate,' he amended easily. 'But, however you like to be called, you still haven't answered my question.'

From cool and collected businesswoman, Kate suddenly found herself plunged into an emotional maelstrom she couldn't contain. 'Well, here's one for you,' she said hotly as she sprang up to confront him. 'Are you trying to tell me that everyone—absolutely everyone else has accepted this *deal*?' The way she stressed the last word turned it into an accusation.

'I'm not trying to tell you anything, Kate,' the Count countered calmly. 'It's a fact. And I'm not offering anyone a deal. I'm making them a fair offer.'

Kate couldn't speak for a moment as she stood mashing her lips together in total impotence while fractured images of blissful childhood holidays flashed behind her eyes—holidays she had naïvely imagined she could recreate. 'I don't believe it,' she said stubbornly.

'Believe it,' he returned steadily. 'The days when holiday homes were an integral part of the Villeneuve estates are in the past.'

'But what about all the other tenants—their relatives—friends?' Kate said heatedly as the eclectic group of characters that used to holiday on the estate each year gathered in her mind. 'Don't you care about them at all?'

'The people to whom I presume you are referring used the cottages as second homes—holiday homes,' he said patiently. 'And without a single exception they were all delighted to accept my offer.'

'Well, I'm not,' Kate said, clenching her fists into balls of frustration.

'You haven't heard what's on offer yet,' he pointed out.

'And I don't need to,' Kate assured him as her heart struggled to accept the fact that she could not hold on to the past by sheer force of will.

'*Ca suffit maintenant!* You must listen to what I have to say, Kate,' he insisted firmly. 'This is a working estate now, not a holiday camp.'

'It never was a holiday camp,' she fired back at him.

'And I seem to remember a time when your family welcomed visitors.' But the heat was seeping out of her attack. He had made it quite clear that there was no crusade for her to embark on—it was far too late for that.

'That may have been true when my father was alive,' he conceded gently. 'But the Villeneuve estates are destined to make a great deal of money now. These vineyards will eventually become some of the most profitable in the world—'

'Money!' Kate muttered angrily as she turned away to lash her arms around her body in a defensive hug. 'Is profit and loss all you care about now?' She swung round to confront him again.

She had always known that once Guy de Villeneuve took over the running of the estates he would make a success of it…of his life…of everything. She pulled her gaze away when she saw that the corners of his mouth were slipping down in a rueful smile.

'I'm sorry you feel like that, Kate,' he said evenly. 'I know money isn't everything. But would you rather the estate went bankrupt…that families who have lived in the village for generations were scattered to the four winds? Because that's where harsh reality was leading. I haven't enjoyed every part of this revival, despite what you think. Yes, sacrifices have had to be made. But something had to give and I was determined it wouldn't be those people who depend on me for their livelihoods.' And, when she didn't reply and only hugged herself closer in the full knowledge that what he was saying made sense, he added softly, 'Think what you will of me, Kate. But the fact remains that times have changed and so have I. And so must you—'

'No!' she flared passionately, suddenly overcome with a great dread of leaving France—of abandoning her hopes, her dreams. The very idea was insupportable. 'Take your wretched ground rent! Ten years in advance if you must! I own the lease on the cottage now and I have no intention of selling it back to you. You'll just have to conduct your business around me.'

'That can be arranged,' he agreed thoughtfully.

Too thoughtfully, Kate realised, even through the red haze of anger that was threatening to engulf her. He seized every barb she flung his way and sent back a rainbow. In that sense if no other nothing had changed between them. She was still the wilful tomboy in thrall to Guy de Villeneuve's mastery. But she was a successful woman now, with her own business empire to run, she reminded herself furiously. And this obduracy on his part was infuriating and unfair. He clearly wasn't going to take her seriously, unless—

'So, you'll conduct your business around me while I carry out my business from the cottage?' she demanded as the need to provoke a reaction overtook her caution. She watched as one of his upswept ebony brows quirked in mild surprise and waited for what she confidently expected would be a huge explosion.

'Your business?' he enquired softly.

'That's what I said.'

But what do you intend to—?'

'Oh, more of the same,' Kate confessed vaguely, flipping her wrist as if what it was need not concern him.

'The same as what, Kate?' he pressed, an ominous note sounding now in his mellow tone. 'Having established that you are in fact the principal shareholder of Freedom Holidays,' he continued, as if reasoning everything through out loud, 'I can hardly imagine that you intend to set up one of your vast Internet travel shops in the heart of the French countryside. Where will you get your customers from? Not to mention your staff—'

'For what I have in mind,' Kate revealed, feeling her confidence growing by the second, 'I am the only member of staff necessary.' She knew she had struck a goal at last and had the satisfaction of seeing his handsome brow pleat in puzzlement.

'But all your other sites are on the high street—'

'No. You're missing the point,' she said, feeling the same rush of excitement she felt each time she contemplated this new turn in her career.

'*Vraiment*, I am?' he said, bringing his brows together to view her through narrowed silver-slit eyes.

'This isn't going to be like my other sites,' she said, struggling to rein back her enthusiasm in case she gave too much away too soon.

'A new venture?'

'You could say that,' she admitted, forced to look away from his sharp stare.

'So, explain what you mean,' he insisted in a tone that was gentle in the same way that he might be gentle with a fishing line before giving it that final tug.

Or gentle like an extremely persuasive and ultimately demanding caress, Kate thought, momentarily losing her train of thought. Changing tack, she went back on the attack.

'That's more than enough information for now,' she said, relishing the unaccustomed sense of having outmanoeuvred him for once. 'I shall expect your people to come tomorrow and pull down all the boards covering my windows, tidy the garden, reconnect the mains services—'

'*Seigneur!* Is that all?'

And now she gave him the full benefit of her confident emerald stare. 'I'm not joking, Guy' she warned. 'I've paid good money for the upkeep of La Petite Maison and now I want to see some results. The whole place is in a chaotic state…and I thought I was paying for—'

'What, Kate?' His eyes were like flint.

Sensation ripped through her—awareness, longing and then finally, after a huge internal battle, resolve. 'You'll see to it?'

'There's hardly any point—'

'No point?'

'I thought I had made myself clear, Kate. There are to be no more holiday homes on the Villeneuve estate—'

'And I thought I made myself equally clear,' Kate returned tensely. 'La Petite Maison is not going to be a holiday home. And, what's more, it's not for sale—to you, or to anyone else.'

'You may come to regret that decision—'

'Are you threatening me, Guy?'

Rather than checking him, this challenge only served to unleash something primal in his gaze, so that what had once been so direct, so uncompromising, grew dangerously hot. Throwing his head back, he loosed a short and very masculine laugh. 'Still so fiery, Kate,' he growled approvingly. 'Still my little spitfire, aren't you, Katie Foster?'

The possessive note in his voice…domination almost, released a tidal wave of longing inside Kate's chest—a tidal wave that swept quickly to inhabit each one of her erotic zones. And not singly, allowing her time to adjust and conceal, but all at once so that she gasped and reddened as instinctively she swayed towards him.

'A spitfire on heat, Katie?' he suggested sardonically as he moved away.

Reduced to shaking her head in violent denial, Kate managed to gasp out a correction on her childhood name at least. But even as she uttered the reprimand she knew by his face that it fell on deaf ears.

'So,' he said, clearly relishing the moment, 'it's good to see that nothing's changed since we last met.'

His arrogance was astounding, but at least it served as a wake-up call.

'You might find that quite a lot has changed in ten years,' Kate said tensely. 'Not least of which is my capacity for standing up for myself.'

'*Excellent,*' he drawled mildly in French. 'I love a good fight.'

His bold stare sent ribbons of fire curling down her spine. She watched transfixed as he reached up to loosen his silk tie with one strong tanned hand and then went on to free a couple of buttons at the neck of his crisp white shirt.

'Maybe some things have changed,' he agreed as he viewed her through storm-grey eyes. 'But, as far as I can see, only for the better.'

Kate tried to look away as he lazily fingered the blue-black stubble shading his jaw but found she couldn't.

'Stop it!' she warned as he prowled a step closer. 'You were wrong about me ten years ago. And you're just as wrong about me now.' She saw his eyes gleam at the recollection.

'Ten years ago there was some excuse for your behaviour,' he said sternly, his mouth curving with pleasure when he saw how easily the authority in his voice melted her. 'You were only sixteen,' he continued relentlessly. 'And, if I remember the occasion correctly, it was you who made a mistake, not me.'

As he exhaled the last words on a sigh of mock-regret the thunderous pulse in her chest moved down to a lower and far more receptive area.

'By imagining you were a gentleman?' she demanded breathlessly, fighting to keep her voice steady as she tried not to betray what was happening.

He shrugged off the insult. 'By imagining I would take advantage of you when you were little more than a child.' As his darkly amused glance swept over her it seemed to confirm that she no longer qualified for this consideration.

'You didn't have to—'

'Didn't have to what?' he cut in. 'Throw you over my shoulder and transport you back to the safety of Madame Broadbent's arms?'

'They were a damn sight safer than yours!' She was unprepared for the sensual onslaught precipitated by the images of that one careless remark. But even remembering her clumsy attempt to make a pass at him all those years ago wasn't to blame for the colour that rushed to her cheeks. It was his friends' faces when Guy had hoisted her into his arms and carried her away from his party and back to her aunt's cottage. She felt the humiliation as keenly now as she had done at the time.

'I'll forget it if you will,' he suggested wryly. 'Shall we start again from scratch?'

'Not a chance!' Kate flared as she struggled to free her mind from the embarrassment. She wasn't expecting him to move at all…let alone so fast. She gasped when he seized hold of her arms in his warm, strong grip.

'Still the same unbroken filly longing for a master to ride her into submission,' he murmured.

The surge of sensation hit with such force that Kate anchored her gaze on the fluttering pennant of a ship under full sail in an undoubtedly priceless oil painting and prayed her knees wouldn't give way.

But the sound of satisfaction that came from somewhere deep in his throat went on teasing her arousal. 'I am not one of your polo ponies,' she managed as he suddenly let her go. 'Don't you dare speak to me like that!'

'I'll speak to you any way I like. And I *dare*,' he said, emphasising the word in a low voice full of amusement, 'because I'm guessing there's still everything to play for.' And then he touched her, running his hands up and down her naked arms with a touch so light it was unbearable, while he watched her trembling with almost clinical interest.

'This isn't a game,' Kate gasped as his hands rested then tightened again on her arms. She knew it was useless to try and pit her strength against his. Since the last time they had seen each other the Count had only grown broader, taller, stronger…and infinitely more desirable. Mashing her lips together fiercely, she refocused fast. Softening in his arms briefly defused his assault and as he released her she reclaimed her professional persona. 'OK,' she said coolly. 'Perhaps you're right. Perhaps we should start afresh.'

The Count acknowledged this apparent change of heart with a thoughtful twist of his sensuous mouth. *'Bien,'* he agreed, viewing her keenly. 'You'd better tell me what you've got in mind.'

# CHAPTER TWO

WHEN Kate left the château she was feeling more battle-shocked than she could ever remember but confident too that she had achieved at least a partial victory; in business that was usually enough for her to lay the foundations for something far more conclusive on the next occasion. The buzz of excitement that always accompanied a hard-won deal was thrumming through every nerve in her body. But was it the deal or something else? Even if her mind was awash with ideas for her new venture now that she had bought herself some time, she couldn't ignore the fact that seeing Guy de Villeneuve again had really shaken her up.

She paused with her hand on the door of her rented Jeep. The meeting had gone better than she might have expected. Guy had agreed to send his men to tear down the last of the wooden boards covering her windows and clear the worst of the weeds and brambles from the garden. He was also going to see about having the mains services reconnected for her, although the vagaries of local bureaucracy meant this might take some time. The fact that he appeared to have accepted she would not be selling the lease of the cottage back to him, but intended to live in it instead, should have been enough for her. But the part of her mind that handled less tangible matters was very badly shaken indeed. She had never come out of a business meeting with nipples so tight they burned. And the very last thing she needed was erotic fantasies taking her eye off the ball when she had no electricity, only a mobile phone and candles, and her first guests arrived in—she pulled a face as she glanced at her wristwatch—a little under three weeks' time!

No. She hadn't been totally straight with Monsieur le

Comte. But Guy's discovery that she intended to live in the cottage had been enough of a shock for him for one day. If he knew she intended to turn the picturesque dwelling into a holiday retreat for exhausted executives… Kate closed her eyes briefly against the image of sheer fury that was conjured up and then firmed her lips determinedly. For now as far as Guy de Villeneuve was concerned, ignorance was bliss.

The customary pin-neat state of Aunt Alice's charming home had lulled her into a false sense of security, Kate realised as she drew to a halt outside the rose-festooned archway marking the cinder path to the front door. Accepting the first bookings had been such a thrill for her she had not even stopped to consider the possibility that everything could deteriorate so quickly. But here in the Garden of France, easily a thousand miles further south than where she lived in England, everything grew so much faster. Even the weeds seemed to possess a special vigour, she noticed as she made her way down the overgrown path. And that was just outside the cottage, she thought ruefully as she slipped the heavy iron key into its impressive lock. Thanks to the boarded-over windows, the hot, airless interior had provided an ideal breeding ground for just about every species of insect she could think of.

Yet even now as the door swung open on its well-oiled hinges she half-expected to find everything unchanged since her last visit. Could that day of laughter and relaxation really have been just six short months ago? There had been no hint of the storm clouds to come…and no Count Guy de Villeneuve to muddy the water. He had yet to return home and claim his inheritance. But everything had changed since the terrible car accident that had killed her aunt and Guy's father, Kate realised, and the sooner she accepted that fact, the better.

As the door shut with a decisive thud she gave in to a great wave of loss, pausing for a moment with her back pressed against the dark polished oak and both her eyes and mind closed against the alteration. The desecration of the cottage was nothing in comparison to the hollow in her heart that used to be filled by a bubbly old lady with sharp, periwinkle-blue eyes. But just thinking about Aunt Alice was enough to invoke her indomitable spirit and, dashing the tears from her face, Kate feasted her eyes on what did remain at La Petite Maison.

Deciding to make a note of every repair that could possibly be needed once the immediate damage was made good, she stepped outside again and stood hands on hips surveying her new domain. Quirky described it to perfection, she decided. Even the higgledy-piggledy roof tiles shaded from deepest coral to palest sand formed a hat several sizes too large for the half-timbered frame. And, since she had torn down the offending boards from two of the front windows, they winked benignly at her like friendly eyes set in whitewashed walls which billowed out in places like plump chalky cheeks. She felt a rush of pride and affection, as if La Petite Maison was a child about to embark upon a new stage in its life, and she the bow from which this arrow would be launched.

She headed off round the side of the building where she had left all the tools she needed to tear down the rest of the wooden panels. Monsieur le Comte might be sending his men over to help tomorrow, but she couldn't wait that long. Entry to the rear of the cottage was gained through a stable-style door and to one side of this stood a tall wooden boot box secured with a black iron bolt. Inside the box she had placed a claw hammer for wrenching free nails and a screwdriver for wiggling inside the panels to loosen them until she could manage to heave them off.

Once she had the tools, Kate set about dislodging a really stubborn strip of wood some vandal from the Villeneuve estate office had seen fit to nail across her kitchen window. She exclaimed with angry surprise as the screwdriver skidded off the smooth surface to land, point down, in the heel of her palm. She was still hopping around cursing loudly when she heard the sound of a horse's hooves crunching briskly along the cinder path that skirted the front garden. 'Oh, no, not visitors!' she grumbled, sucking hard on her damaged hand. Then, shooting upright, she thrust the same hand behind her back as both horse and rider came into view. 'Guy!' she exclaimed, affecting an expression somewhere between righteous surprise and modest unpreparedness for greeting the Lord of the Manor. 'What brings you here?'

'I wanted to see the cottage for myself,' he said springing down from an edgy looking bay. 'What have you done?' he demanded, not fooled by her play-acting for a minute.

Kate looked on warily as he snatched off a pair of well-worn riding gloves and slipped them into the back pocket of his breeches. Then, pausing only to throw the reins over the horse's neck, he strode over to her, seized her arm and examined her hand.

'I'm fine. It's nothing—nothing,' Kate insisted as she tried to free herself.

'Hold still,' he insisted irritably. 'You've punctured the skin. Is your tetanus shot up to date?'

'Yes,' she said, wincing as he subjected the tender spot to some more probing.

'Antiseptic inside?'

Aunt Alice had scored A star in practicalities. There was everything that could possibly be needed to deal with any home emergency inside the locked cupboard in the bathroom.

'No,' Kate said, as visions of Le Comte in knee-length black leather boots striding around the bedroom area swam into her mind.

'No first aid kit?' he demanded impatiently.

'I've been far too busy trying to undo all the damage here to be concerned about—'

'Your safety?'

'Guy, I—'

'What?' he said fiercely, keeping a firm hold of her when she struggled to pull away. 'What would you like to say to me, Kate?'

His voice was demanding and full of an intensity she hadn't heard before. Her hand hurt like hell. And the fact that it was he who sounded furious when it was she who had every right to be angry, filled her with a heat so profound that for that moment she lost all hold on reason.

'Don't you dare shout at me!' she raged, thumping his chest with her free hand. But, instead of shouting back, he only laughed as he grabbed her flailing arm and held her close. So close she was rammed against his chest where the steady rhythm of his heart throbbed in her ears and the comfortingly fresh scent of clean brushed cotton and warm hard man worked some sort of magic on her agitated mind.

'Better?' he murmured, stroking her head.

Confused, distressed, but spent, she moved her head slightly in agreement. 'It hurts,' she admitted. And if he thought she meant her hand then that was for the best. But when Guy held her in his arms the same longings that had made her teenage years such misery rose up again to taunt her with the unbridgeable gap between them.

It wasn't just the twelve years or so that separated them by age, but the wealth of experience possessed by a man like the Count. And the years of separation only seemed to have given that impression strength, as if it had been resting dormant like some forgotten seed. They were as far apart as ever…perhaps more so, because now they were adults with their own lives to lead and sooner rather than later, Guy, Comte de Villenueve was going to discover that she had misled him badly.

He released her after a couple of minutes, but only to arm's length. 'Are you sure there's nothing in the cottage we can treat your hand with?'

Kate missed a beat as she considered how to stop him going inside without being downright rude. She wasn't ready for visitors yet, especially not Guy. Until every single detail inside the cottage had been returned to the way that she wanted it...remembered it, no one was going to get past that door.

'No. I cleared everything out. Past the sell-by date.' She held her arms open in a gesture of helpless regret. 'Don't worry. I'll go to the *pharmacie* in the village.'

He still looked unconvinced. 'I'll take you.'

'No. Don't be silly, I—' But he wouldn't let go of her wrist, and they were already halfway across the yard before she realised what was happening. Lifting her up, he swung her on to his horse's back, and moments later, he was seated behind her with his free arm banded around her waist.

'Don't worry, I'll take it easy,' he promised, nudging the horse into a gentle walk.

The fact that she hadn't ridden since childhood was nothing to fear in comparison to the touch of Guy's warm arm about her. And it was no good trying to keep a safe distance from him when he only yanked her back again.

'Relax,' he murmured so close to her ear that she shivered involuntarily. 'You're making him nervous.'

The horse's sensibilities were the last thing on Kate's mind, but the relaxed clip-clop was certainly going some way to soothing her shattered nerves. Soon she was swaying easily in time to the rhythm of the stallion's hooves and the earlier rigidity gave way to what she managed to convince herself was a far more natural posture—resting close up to Guy.

'Where are we going?' As she turned to ask the question her cheek encountered the rugged planes of his beard-roughened face. It felt good. Scratchy, but good. And the heat that collected instantly in her cheeks moved quickly on to more erogenous zones so that she savoured the effect of Guy's muscle-corded forearm against her sensitive nipples and even relished the movement of the horse as he held her firmly in place on the saddle.

'Does it hurt?'

His murmured question trespassed on these sensual indulgences so that she felt vulnerable and guilty, as if she was a child again and he had caught her out doing something naughty. 'It's not too bad now,' she said huskily. 'Why?'

'I heard you sigh. I just wondered—'

He let the sentence hang as he waited for her explanation. 'Where are we going, Guy?' she said, forcing some focus back into her voice.

'Château…*pharmacie*,' he said casually. 'Your choice.'

'*Pharmacie*,' Kate said quickly.

'As you wish,' he agreed evenly, turning the horse on to a right-hand fork in the road.

'At least there Monsieur Dupont, the *pharmacien* can take a look at it,' Kate pointed out, trying to excuse her reluctance to place herself on Guy's territory—under his control. She shook her head in an effort to banish all wayward thoughts concerning Guy once and for all.

He made a sound of agreement low down in his chest and tightened his arm a fraction. 'Are you ready to go faster?'

Any faster than this and she would not be held responsible for the consequences, Kate thought.

Taking her silence for assent, Guy shortened the reins and took the wilful stallion in a firmer grip between his thighs. With barely an aid, as far as Kate could detect, he brought the horse from a brisk walk to a steady canter, holding her all the while, easily, but firmly, so that she never felt in danger once—from falling off, at least.

The Count de Villeneuve's status in the village was never clearer than when he put in a personal appearance, Kate realised as people turned to wave and call out greetings.

But rather than the type of sycophantic attention she might have expected a member of the aristocracy to attract, he was accorded the most genuine warmth and respect. On top of this she soon realised that he possessed an encyclopaedic knowledge of village life. There didn't appear to be one family with which he was not acquainted, one difficulty of which he was not aware, or one successful enterprise in which he did not have at least a passing interest.

'How do you know so much about so many people?' Kate asked after one particularly dynamic encounter that had involved arranging a match between a neighbouring village and the Villeneuve *pétanque* team.

His faintly bemused eyes clashed with hers. 'I make it my business to know,' he explained. 'This isn't a hobby for me, Kate. This village…these people are my life.'

How she envied them.

Like most of the shops in the village, the same family had run the *pharmacie* for generations. Monsieur Dupont, *le pharmacien*, a short wiry man with a mischievous smile hidden behind his pebble glasses, was all bristling moustache and plastered down hair. When he saw his latest customers he made a little jump in order to attract their attention over the phalanx of waiting customers who took up several rows in front of the mahogany framed glass-topped counter where he was holding court. Silence fell like a blanket as everyone turned to stare.

'Monsieur le Comte,' the pharmacist exclaimed. '*Quel honneur!* What can I do for you?'

'See to everyone else first,' Guy insisted. 'I think the emergency has passed.' He looked at Kate for confirmation.

'I'm fine, honestly,' she insisted in a self-conscious whisper. 'I could probably pick up some antiseptic and a bandage at the *supermarché*.

'*Supermarché!*' Monsieur Dupont exclaimed, throwing up his hands in horror. 'The very idea! Clear the way, everyone!' he insisted, conducting his crowd of customers with the finesse of a maestro. 'Let the young lady come forward.'

'No, really, there's no need for this,' Kate protested as Guy led her to the front of the counter.

'Humour him,' Guy whispered, unaware that his warm breath was all it took to raise the fine hairs on the back of her neck. 'He's only trying to help.'

Conscious that now she was the centre of attention, Kate put a brave face on it and walked up to the counter.

'Now then, let me see, *mademoiselle*,' Monsieur Dupont said as he paid her the ultimate compliment of leaving his post to come around the counter into the main body of the shop.

Before she could stop him, Guy had taken hold of her arm and was holding out her hand for the dapper older man to examine. The rest of the customers formed an arc around them as they waited in breathless anticipation for Monsieur Dupont's diagnosis.

'Nasty,' he began as he peered myopically at Kate's hand. 'Slight abrasion.' He turned her hand carefully in front of him, pulling his spectacles down on to the very end of his nose to take a closer look. 'Bruising…painful no doubt…but fortunately no deep wound,' he proclaimed to sighs all round. 'Not a horse-riding accident, I hope, *mademoiselle*?' he teased, winking at Guy and then glancing at the stallion tethered to the rail outside his shop. Every head in the place turned to follow his gaze and one by one some of the older women broke into delighted laughter embroidered by a round of eloquent nudges.

'Not a horse-riding accident,' Kate confirmed, feeling her face flush as she realised what people must be thinking.

'Hold her steady while I bathe the wound, if you please, Monsieur le Comte,' the pharmacist instructed Guy. 'This may sting a little, *mademoiselle*,' he confided in Kate. 'And I wouldn't like her to pull away,' he added in a dramatic stage whisper.

'Don't worry, *monsieur*,' Guy assured the jaunty pharmacist. 'I won't let her get away.'

Kate's heart started beating to its own crazy rhythm. And it was a rhythm that had nothing to do with stinging wounds or the unselfconscious scrutiny of anyone in the shop.

Monsieur Dupont was determined to draw out the drama to its fullest extent and was brandishing a length of bandage that could have easily bound her up like an Egyptian mummy from top to toe. 'Now you may release her,' he informed Guy. 'The unpleasant part is over—'

This time he was wrong, Kate thought as Guy let her go. As far as she was concerned, the pleasant part was over. She was conscious of Guy watching her, leaning back casually against the wall with his arms loosely folded and one tightly clad leg crossed nonchalantly over the other.

'There!' Monsieur Dupont declared with a flourish. 'A neat job, if I say so myself.'

'A very neat job,' Guy confirmed as he eased himself away from the wall. 'What do I owe you, Monsieur Dupont?'

'Owe me!'

Kate felt sure that all the women in the shop tensed and leaned forward a little to catch him, so great was Monsieur Dupont's affront.

'I want nothing from you, *monsieur*, except your assurances that you will escort this young lady home. She's had quite a shock today.'

Understatement of the year! Kate thought wryly as Guy accepted the gesture with his customary charm.

'I'm sure there must be something I can do in return for you,' he insisted.

'Monsieur le Comte,' Monsieur Dupont exclaimed bashfully with a very low bow indeed, 'I assure you, there is no need whatever—'

'I have a better idea,' Kate broke in impulsively. 'In

about three weeks' time I intend to have a house-warming—' Well, that was one way of describing the opening of her guest house and the safest option whilst Guy was around. 'I'd like to invite you...all—' She caught sight of Guy's face and stopped.

'I hope that includes me,' he said.

Her mouth dried.

'*Mademoiselle* could not possibly leave you out, Monsieur le Comte,' Monsieur Dupont exclaimed as he turned from one to the other like a spectator at a tennis match. 'Well, could you, *mademoiselle*?'

'No, of course not. You're very welcome, Guy.'

'You don't sound too sure,' he murmured so that only she could hear. 'Don't forget to send that invitation.'

'I won't,' Kate promised, backing her way towards the entrance. 'Well, thank you, Monsieur Dupont...everyone... Guy.'

'Not so fast,' Guy drawled, coming after her. 'I have to see you home, remember?'

'I can manage...honestly,' she protested when he insisted on guiding her out by the elbow. 'I can walk.'

'So can I,' he pointed out. 'Or we can ride back. It's entirely up to you.'

'You don't have to treat me like a child. I hurt my hand, that's all. It's been attended to. Thank you very much for your assistance—'

'*Et au revoir?*' he suggested sardonically.

'Yes. No,' Kate amended quickly, realising how ungrateful he must think her.

'Walk, or ride?' he demanded.

The day had mellowed into a hazy, lazy afternoon and in spite of all the warning klaxons sounding in her head, Kate chose to walk. She waited outside under the green and white striped awning of the *pharmacie* until Guy found one of the young village lads to ride his horse back to the stables at the château.

'You're very trusting,' she said, seeing the young boy's face light up with excited anticipation as he urged the magnificent animal into a brisk trot.

'Yes, aren't I?' Guy agreed dryly. 'But since I've known Leon since birth, as I have all the youngsters in the village, I'd say it was a calculated risk. I didn't pick him out at random. He is one of the best young riders we have around here. Letting him ride Fireflash is my way of showing my appreciation for the hours he puts into his training.'

'I'm sorry. That was clumsy of me. I should have realised—'

'Forget it,' Guy said, steering her in the direction of the shops.

'Where are we going now?' she demanded when he paused to stare into the window of the *patisserie*.

'Cake? No,' he said, reading her face. 'I take you for a bread, cheese and salad woman right now.'

'And what's that supposed to mean?' Kate asked suspiciously.

'Cake signals self-indulgence to me. Not that there's anything wrong with that, but, right now, you strike me as being in a rolling up your sleeves kind of a mood.'

'Hardly,' Kate said, struggling to rein in her wayward senses as she raised her bandaged hand to make the point.

'Well, as I suppose I'm indirectly responsible for that, how about I do the labouring and you give the orders?'

'Count Guy de Villeneuve labouring?' Kate exclaimed as she threw him a look.

'I am quite a capable individual,' he confided, moving in close. 'Believe it or not, I can even put jam on my own croissant in the morning.'

As his breath warmed her ear, Kate backed away. 'Please stop teasing me, Guy.'

'Why?' he murmured. 'You used to love it when you were a little girl.'

Her heart thundered at the reminder. Once any attention

from the handsome young aristocrat had been bliss, but
now it only spelled trouble.

'What do we need food for anyway?' she said, trying to
keep her mind from straying on to dangerous territory.

'I get very hungry when I work.'

'You're not going to be doing any work,' Kate insisted
firmly. Her original resolution still held firm. No one was
setting foot inside the cottage until she was completely satisfied that the interior had been returned to its original pristine condition—and that included Guy. No, especially Guy,
she thought, shooting a glance at him. 'So, you don't need
to eat.'

'Nonsense!' he said, steering her into the *fromagerie*.
'I'm hungry. We'll have a picnic.'

Kate sighed with frustration. And she'd thought she was
self-willed! She hadn't known the meaning of that state
until now!

At least she succeeded in getting her own way over one
thing. Pleading a muddle at the cottage, she set out the food
Guy insisted on buying for them on the grassy bank above
the narrow stream that meandered through the garden. And
somehow the years seemed to peel away until it was almost
like being back in the time when groups of holidaymakers,
villagers, estate workers and even members of Guy's own
family had congregated on the banks of the main river that
ran through the town to loll away the sunny afternoons
eating and chatting. But then Guy wouldn't always have
chosen to sit with her…or, more precisely, lie by her side,
Kate realised as she took the greaseproof wrapping paper
off the cheese. The bread shop had furnished her with a red
gingham cloth and a wicker basket in which to put the
mountain of food Guy had acquired on his trawl round the
village square. There was chilled wine, a fragrant crusty
loaf, some fat green olives and a selection of cheeses to
arrange on top of the makeshift table she had adapted from
a tree stump.

Removing a graceful strand of meadow grass from his mouth, Guy rolled over on to his side. Resting his head on the heel of his hand, he gazed up at her. 'Ready yet?' he murmured. 'I'm starving.'

'Ready,' Kate confirmed, feeling her face growing hot beneath his scrutiny. He looked gorgeous, she realised, trying to find comfort in the fact that he seemed so at ease...deceptively so, she warned herself, and not a moment too soon.

'Feed me,' he called across to her in a softly seductive voice.

'Get it yourself,' Kate blurted, too shaken to realise she had reverted to the way she might have spoken to him when she was a cheeky teenager.

Picking up on her mood, Guy countered by falling back into the role he had once played in her life...and it was a dangerously provocative role that carried far more risk than the sophisticated manner that had marked his behaviour towards her since her return.

'It's a no to that, Katie Foster,' he drawled lazily. 'You feed me, or you pay the penalty. You owe me a favour. And now I'm calling it in.'

Guy's apparent languor didn't fool Kate for a moment. He was just as likely to launch himself on her at any moment and tickle her to death, she remembered, trying not to let her disappointment at the likely outcome become too apparent.

'I need to build up my strength for the hard work to come,' he reasoned, tossing a languid glance towards the cottage.

Kate doubted that, judging by the muscles bulging beneath the pewter-coloured polo shirt he was wearing...and his thighs. She dragged her eyes up again, conscious that he was still watching her. 'Don't worry about that now, Guy,' she said, forcing her attention back to more mundane problems. 'There's really no need if your men are coming tomorrow—'

'I can't allow you to go another day with boards across the windows,' he insisted. 'It's intolerable.' His voice grew harsh, as if they had both returned at the same time from their brief visit to the past. 'If I'd had any idea at all that you were trying to live here—'

'I haven't been here all that long.'

'It doesn't matter,' he said firmly. 'It must have been a shock for you finding the cottage in this condition.' He sat up abruptly and levelled a penetrating stare straight into her eyes. 'And on top of everything else—' He pressed his beautifully shaped lips together as he shook his head. 'Please accept my apologies.'

'Accepted,' Kate said as she broke the bread into chunks. She wasn't sure which was safer—Guy playful or Guy serious.

'So now you can feed me,' he murmured, rolling on to his back again.

Kate's hands remained suspended in mid-air. For a moment it seemed as if the bees stopped humming and the soft breeze rustling through the leaves died away. Then Guy's laugh splintered her trance.

'Hurry up, Kate. Or I'll just have to come over there and make you,' he warned.

Kate's eyes cleared and the soundscape burst into life again. 'You wouldn't,' she said confidently.

*'Vraiment?'* he countered softly.

Before his intentions could be put to the test, she switched to a subject that was both important to her and safe. 'Guy, I know I've only just arrived. But, if it's possible, I would like to make arrangements to see your mother.'

His mood altered in an instant. 'She isn't seeing anyone.'

'Are you quite sure she wouldn't see me?'

'Anything that reminds her of the accident— And in particular anything that reminds her of her dearest friend, your aunt—'

'I understand,' Kate broke in softly. 'I'd just like her to know that I was asking after her, that I'm thinking about her. You will tell her that?'

'*Naturellement,*' he said. 'And thank you, Kate. It's very good of you to be so concerned. I think she gets very lonely up at the château. As soon as she feels up to it I'll suggest that you pay her a visit.'

'Or she's always welcome here at La Petite Maison,' Kate said quickly. 'At least when everything's back to normal,' she qualified. 'I'd hate her to see the cottage as it is right now.'

A muscle worked in Guy's jaw as he sprang to his feet. 'Now you're making me feel guilty,' he said, coming over to help her with the food. 'If I had even suspected you meant to come back—'

'Don't,' Kate said firmly. 'It's not all your fault.'

'Well, I'll just have to keep a closer eye on my estate manager in future,' he said. 'It seems my request to dispose of the holiday cottages was handled with more rigour than I had bargained for.'

'I'm sure that's the way business is usually conducted,' Kate said wryly. 'I know I won't brook any time-wasting once I set my sights on achieving a certain goal.'

'But this isn't business,' Guy pointed out as he cut a slab of creamy Brie and pressed it into the soft heart of the fresh bread for her. 'It's you.'

His eyes were dancing with laughter. At her? With her? Kate had no idea as she took the bread from him and sucked her thumb appreciatively. 'This is delicious.'

'I couldn't agree more,' Guy murmured as he poured them both a glass of chilled white wine.

After the picnic Guy insisted on staying on until he had removed every single board from her windows. And he promised that his workmen would bring tubs of plastic wood with them to repair any holes made by the nails. Then the decorators would arrive.

Waving him off, Kate decided that the cottage would be back to normal in no time. Except that it never would be completely back to normal, she thought wistfully, taking the wicker trug laden with flowers they had collected inside with her. Her intention was to keep everything just as it had been during Aunt Alice's lifetime. A memorial? No, a tribute, she corrected herself as she dropped the bunch of garden blooms into a vase of water. And when Guy found out what she really planned to do with La Petite Maison? She would have found the opportunity to explain her plans to him long before that became a problem, she told herself confidently.

# CHAPTER THREE

IT WAS deep in the still and secret part of the night when time had no meaning that Kate woke up coughing. Reaching out still half-asleep for the switch on the lamp by her bed, she suddenly realised that her eyes were stinging too. Squinting her eyes as she peered at the clock she became slowly conscious of the sharp, throat-catching tang of fire. She could taste it, smell it…and, as if drawn by an invisible hand to contemplate the dawning horror, she could see it too as her eyes fixed on the bottom of the heavy oak door where the first few puffs were billowing innocently through a tiny gap at the base.

Instantly alert, she sprang out of bed and raced to grab her robe. Returning to the door, she felt down the length of it with the flat of her hand. It was still cool and formed a sturdy barrier between her and whatever lay beyond. She stiffened, listening intently as she tried to gauge the extent of the fire. Her face tensed with concern. She could hear the crackling of the flames quite clearly. But she had been so careful…

Obviously not careful enough, she thought, remembering the candles she had lit on the kitchen table. Recreating the scene in her mind, she pictured the photograph albums next to the candles. She had meant to move them before going to bed. But she had stayed up too long worrying about Guy, her mixed-up feelings, the state of the cottage and whether she could possibly get it ready in time for her first guests. A sharp sound of distress escaped from her throat as she realised that would never happen now. And if by some miracle it did? Guy would never forgive her either way. She had lied to him. And she had planned to coax Guy's

45

elderly mother out of isolation too, bring her to the cottage… Was this like drowning, she wondered, having your whole life flash before your eyes?

Kate forced her attention back to the door. One thing was for sure; she had wasted enough time. Opening the door a crack, she stared into the smoke-filled gloom. The stairs were still clear and probably safe. Glancing behind her into the bedroom, she took the chance to go back and snatch up a couple of things.

On the glass-covered surface of the bow-fronted dressing table sat a silver frame containing a photograph of Aunt Alice, and to either side of Aunt Alice like two disapproving sentinels stood Kate's mother and father. Clutching the frame in one hand, she snatched up a silver locket. The locket contained a photograph of herself as a young child staring defiantly into the camera. Kate felt a sudden pang to see that at nine years old there had already been something pinched and anxious behind her bravado. Snub-nosed and freckled and with a halo of red-gold curls in such disarray it proved that the photograph could only have been taken in France. And on the facing side, in perfect counterbalance to the reckless young hoyden she had once been, Aunt Alice appeared, apple-cheeked and twinkling. The locket had no real value except that it expressed everything about her young life and the influence Aunt Alice had wielded upon it…and that made it one of her most treasured possessions. She never went anywhere without it, for in spite of the angst behind the tomboy façade, those two photographs represented everything that had been good and happy and carefree about her childhood once her parents had agreed that she could be released into Aunt Alice's care each summer.

The smoke was growing dangerously thick and Kate knew she would have to find some clean air or fall where she stood.

This time when she opened the door the heat scorched her face, forcing her to draw back in alarm. Snatching another glance, she saw the fire licking up the sides of the wooden staircase, creating a surreal vista of shadows and flame and smoke and ash. Gathering her courage around her like an invisible blanket, she burst out of the door and with gravity as her only guide she launched herself down the stairs. Her eyes were stinging so badly they filled with tears, blinding her as the thick black smoke curled its deadly tentacles around her chest.

Stumbling across the kitchen she found the back door, but fear made her clumsy as she struggled to pull back the locks. Gasping, coughing and sobbing all at once, only sheer bloody-mindedness kept her going. As the locks yielded she fell into the night and half-crawling scrambled along the path until she could no longer feel the heat of the fire. But as her mind slowly cleared she realised that somehow during her flight the precious locket had fallen from her hand. Her cry of despair sounded eerie in the darkness. But when she turned her agonised gaze on the cottage she saw that smoke was already billowing from the roof and glowing cinders were issuing in burnished clouds through the kitchen window like some unseasonable firework display.

Laughing hysterically, Kate got to her knees and made a desperate calculation. There was no sign as yet of any flames on the upper floor of the cottage. Perhaps she could retrace her steps? Dazed with shock, she got up slowly. She had seen films where people wet a cloth and tied it around their mouth and nose to keep out the worst of the deadly fumes.

All she could think about was the locket. And then she remembered the chain biting into her hand as she leaped down the stairs. Slipping off her robe, she soaked it under the outside tap. Then, shivering with fear and cold, she forced her arms back inside the sodden towelling. Stepping quickly out of her flimsy pyjama bottoms, she wet them too and, tying them around her face, she staggered back to the front door cursing the fact that while her resolve was

as strong as ever, the old injury to her leg was holding her
back. Darting her head in and out fast, she took in the
scene. The fire had taken a strong hold, but the flames
would light her way and she might be all right if she was
quick enough. There was a slim chance she could save the
locket before it melted into a pool of molten metal…and a
slim chance was enough.

She was just gearing herself up to dive in when the sound
of noisy engines crested the ugly sounds of the fire. People
were shouting and then she became aware that alarm bells
were ringing in the village. Relief burst from her throat in
a guttural cry she would not have recognised as her own.
She was so thankful not to be alone—so grateful someone
had noticed and had thought to rouse help. But she was
past the point where reason governed her actions. And if
she was going to find the locket she had to go now—

'No! Kate, no! What are you doing?'

An iron band snapped round her waist, holding her back.
Then she was yanked away from the threshold of the cottage—carried off, away from the stream of people who
were racing up the path—some carrying a wide bore hose
between them, others bringing water in an endless stream
of buckets and all of them shouting, urging each other on
as they rushed to help.

'Let me go! Let me go!' Kate shrieked so forcefully that
her throat was almost raw by the time Guy lowered her to
the ground.

'*Mon Dieu!* Kate!' he said as he stared into her wild,
desperate eyes. 'What were you thinking of? You could
have been killed!'

'I don't care! It doesn't matter! Don't you understand?'
she cried huskily as she tried to fight him off, tried to get
back to the cottage. 'I have to go back. Let me go!'

'No!' Guy rasped as he held her tight to his chest.

'I'm warning you—' But her voice was wobbling and
her legs were giving way.

'No,' he said again a little more gently, but holding her

even more securely. 'You're not going back in there, Kate. It's too late.'

'No! It can't be!' Her cry was almost primeval in intensity. But her ferocity only seemed to make Guy all the more determined to hold on to her.

'*Regardes*, Kate!' he insisted, gripping her chin and forcing her round to face him. 'They're getting the fire under control. The cottage will be saved. Look!' he said again. And when she tried in a last desperate flurry of blows to fight him off, he bound her so tight in his arms she couldn't move at all. 'You can't turn away,' he said, 'and you will listen to me. I will personally oversee all the repairs. I'll have the damn cottage rebuilt brick by brick if necessary. I'll even build it myself—'

'No…no, you don't understand,' she broke in, repeatedly shaking her head. 'It won't be the same.'

'What do you mean, it won't be the same?'

'Aunt Alice's things—' Kate broke off then, sobbing against him, melting into him, accepting, needing his arms around her and the comfort of his soft, body-warmed sweater against her face.

'Things?' Guy queried softly, nestling his face against the top of her head while he smoothed her hair with long calming strokes.

'You know what I mean,' Kate insisted.

'I'm not sure I do,' he said, holding her back so that he could look into her face. 'But if you're trying to tell me that all these tears are being wasted on a few ornaments and decorations—' He shook his head as he stared down at her. Then, very gently, he rested the palm of his right hand against the left side of her chest. 'Aunt Alice is in here, Kate, not in the cottage,' he said softly.

For a few moments she stared back at him. His conviction gave her strength, broke through the madness of the last hour. Very slowly she relaxed in his arms. 'You're right,' she whispered, fighting to come to terms with it. 'But it's not fair,' she added brokenly, half to herself. 'I can't keep hold of the past, however hard I try.'

The soft knit of his cashmere sweater felt warm against her face as she nestled against it and Guy's voice was like a caress as he drew her into him. 'The future will be even better,' he said roughly. 'You'll see.' But then they were distracted by a small group of men, their faces smoke-blackened as they emerged from the cottage.

'Everything is under control, Monsieur le Comte,' said one. 'But we will have a better idea if the structure is safe in the morning, when we can make a thorough examination in good light.'

'Merci…merci beaucoup,' Guy exclaimed softly, still with his arm around Kate, supporting her. 'You have all responded magnificently. I can't thank you enough.'

Kate knew words were inadequate for what they had done. 'You saved the cottage and my life. I will always be in your debt,' she managed huskily.

'It is nothing, mademoiselle,' the leader informed her. It is our job, after all.'

'It was the middle of the night,' Kate pointed out hoarsely. 'Yet you came…all of you.' She turned to include the many villagers who had turned out to help their local firemen.

'Monsieur le Comte alerted us,' one man explained. 'We all rely on each other here in Villeneuve. It's a good system, don't you think, mademoiselle?'

'I certainly do,' she said, flashing a look at Guy, who showed no sign of wanting to accept any of the credit for saving her life. 'And now that the fire is out, can I just go back inside and——?'

'Certainly not, mademoiselle,' the chief fireman insisted. 'We cannot be sure yet that the cottage is safe. You really must wait until tomorrow.'

'But if I only take a quick look around outside, surely that will be OK?' As Guy groaned with impatience she saw how the thick black smudges only managed to enhance his incredible bone structure. Only Guy, she thought ruefully, could look like some warrior prince with what looked like camouflage paint striped across his face.

'You're not going back,' he said bluntly.

Kate bristled. She wasn't used to following orders. 'But if the fire engine turned so that its lights—'

'I know you've had a frightening experience and I know you're upset,' Guy told her, 'but you're not thinking straight. These men left their beds to come here.'

A rush of heat spread across her cheeks as Kate realised he was right. 'I'm sorry,' she said at once. 'It can wait.' It couldn't, but she knew it would have to.

With their job completed, the villagers and the firemen began to peel away, singly and in groups, until just Kate and Guy were left together on the grassy bank in front of the cottage. The only light came from the slivers of moonshine that managed to penetrate the thick canopy of trees.

'I'm taking you home with me,' he said, starting to lead her away.

'Oh, no, I—' She tried to pull back and then stopped. What was she going to do? She had nothing with her and was only wearing the top of her pyjamas under a filthy, wet robe. She could hardly bed down in the forest dressed like that.

'Until we know the cottage is safe you cannot even start to repair…redecorate, let alone move back in. It may be quite some time before it is fit for habitation,' Guy said as he gave her an encouraging nudge towards the path.

Kate grimaced. The shock had put everything out of her head. But this was hardly the time to tell Guy that the cottage had to be ready in under three weeks' time because that was when her first guests arrived.

'Come on,' he said, urging her to keep in step with him. 'You're shivering. And it's not that cold. If you're in shock the sooner I can put you to bed the better.'

'At the château?'

'Of course at the château, where else?' he said speeding up.

'I'm being a terrible nuisance,' Kate said, forced to jog to keep up with him.

'No more than I remember,' he murmured dryly as he steered her through the trees and back on to the path that led to his home.

Being treated like a dainty porcelain doll that might break if it was handled too roughly was something new for Kate. But that was exactly how Madame Duplessis, Guy's formidable housekeeper, insisted she had to be looked after. It was she who had opened the magnificent double doors for them just before dawn that morning, already dressed in her customary uniform of crisply tailored shirt-waister dress, a garment Kate remembered she possessed in any number of sober colours. Clucking with alarm when she had seen the state Kate was in, Madame Duplessis had whisked her away from Guy, insisting she took a warm bath before installing her in one of the sumptuous guest bedrooms. Here Kate had been force-fed with a cup of hot milk, having first been clothed in a floor-length fleecy robe in a soft shade of coral and a long-sleeved cotton nightdress buttoned up to the neck.

If she hadn't been suffering such emotional turmoil she might actually have enjoyed the pampering. Instead, she found herself sitting up in a bed made for Daddy Bear, plucking at the sheets and fretting. At least she had extracted a promise from Guy that, whatever happened, he would take her back to the cottage later that morning... The thought of that alone was enough to send her pulse-rate soaring. But first they had to give Madame Duplessis the slip. As far as that redoubtable lady was concerned, Kate would need to convalesce at Château Villeneuve for the next few months after the terrible shock she had sustained.

Just being close to Guy was therapeutic enough, but there

were other consolations too, Kate mused as she gazed out through one of the tall sash windows by her bed. From her eyrie high in one of the pink-roofed fairytale towers, she had the most magnificent view over the formal gardens at the front of the château, laid out centuries earlier, in homage to Versailles.

The sound of fountains playing in the background was just audible above the steady hum of gardening implements. The team of gardeners had been hard at work since dawn, ensuring that everything was maintained in the pristine condition demanded by the intricate design. But it hadn't always been like this, Kate remembered. When she was small, the gardens had been overgrown and disorganised like every other part of the estate. Guy's father might have been known as the most charming aristocrat in France, but he had also been the most impractical. She could see that Guy had inherited not only the best of his father's qualities, but some other genes that had driven him to restore his ramshackle birthplace as soon as he was able to. He had already explained how he was using ancient plans and drawings whenever possible in order to ensure authenticity and that it was a project that would take him many years to complete.

Her thoughts were interrupted by a knock on the door and her heart shot into overdrive as she watched it swing open. But it was only a young maid in a sky-blue and white gingham dress who had come to collect the breakfast tray. As the girl prepared to shut the door behind her with the tray balanced on one hip, she paused.

'Monsieur le Comte sends his compliments, *mademoiselle*. He hopes you slept well and will see you in the gazebo at noon, if that is convenient to you.'

Kate felt her face flush pink at the prospect. 'It is convenient,' she confirmed, willing her voice to remain steady. 'And thank you for the breakfast,' she called as the girl backed out.

'*Ce n'est rien, mademoiselle.*'

'Oh, there is one thing more,' Kate said, remembering that she had arrived in a filthy bathrobe and the top of her pyjamas. 'I don't suppose there are any clothes I could borrow? Just until I return home.'

The maid's smile grew wider. 'But *mademoiselle*, Monsieur le Comte has arranged everything for you. You will find all you need in the dressing room adjoining your bathroom.'

'Of course,' Kate said hesitantly.

'I hope you like the clothes, *mademoiselle*. A courier arrived with an exquisite selection from the latest collections only minutes ago,' the maid revealed shyly. 'Monsieur le Comte surprised us—' She stopped abruptly, perhaps thinking she had overstepped the mark.

'Go on,' Kate prompted with a smile. 'You can't stop now.'

'Well, we thought them very pretty, *mademoiselle*…and you know men and shopping.' She lifted her shoulders in an elegant little shrug.

'Yes,' Kate agreed, raising her eyebrows in amusement. 'I know just what you mean.'

The fact that everyone was gossiping about her hardly mattered, Kate thought. She would be gone soon enough, and Guy would no doubt have some far more sophisticated companion in her place. But for now she was going to revel in her time at the château. Of course she had been to 'the big house' before, as Aunt Alice had quaintly referred to the colossal and utterly magnificent edifice that was Château Villeneuve. But Kate had never expected to sleep beneath its roof…or one of its many roofs, she mused, smiling as she tried to count exactly how many upside-down rose-tinted ice cream cones there were…

For her part, she had always thought of the château as Sleeping Beauty's palace, and as a little girl had fantasised about her leading role in the drama of life there. What a shame there were no fairy tales for grown ups, she mused with a wry smile. But, even if there had been, everyone knew there was no possibility of fairy tales ever coming true. If that was the case the fire would never have happened, she would be wearing Aunt Alice's locket around her neck and Guy would know her true intentions for La Petite Maison…

Was there a way round the problem? It had been bad enough getting his permission to live in the cottage. If he imagined for one moment that she intended turning it into a guest house… After everything he had done for her she hated herself for deceiving him. And the longer that deception was allowed to continue, the harder it would be to tell him the truth.

Shaking herself out of the doldrums, Kate slipped out of bed. Lifting the telephone, she waited a few moments for Madame Duplessis to answer. 'Do you think it would be possible for me to make a short visit with the Comtesse de Villeneuve today? I see, Madame Duplessis. No matter,' she said after a short pause. 'I will wait for another time, when it is more convenient. Please tell the Countess that Kate Foster was asking about her and sends her love—'

Guy was waiting for her just inside the gazebo with his back turned. Kate was light-footed but he seemed to sense her presence and turned abruptly as she reached the top step.

'Kate!'

The force of his smile competed with the rush of pleasure she felt just seeing him again.

'I take it you slept well, if only for a few hours?'

'You have the most comfortable beds in the entire world. How could I not?'

'I hope you will not be a stranger here at Château Villeneuve now that you have returned to France,' he said formally and with the suggestion of a bow.

'Thank you,' Kate returned with matching decorum. 'And thank you for the beautiful clothes. There was really no need—'

'Forgive me if I disagree,' Guy insisted, walking towards

her. 'I find this season's Chanel so much more appealing than last year's grubby robe.'

His eyes were dark and luminous as he stared into her face and Kate felt as if her racing heart had taken a flying leap into her throat.

'In this instance—' she said wryly '—I think I can safely say you're right.'

'Well, that's a first,' he murmured. 'Do a twirl,' he suggested. 'I'd like to see the full effect of that beautiful dress.'

Kate's brows rose fractionally before she obeyed. But Guy didn't make her feel like a clothes-horse, he made her feel like a valued, cosseted... She actually stamped her foot as she ground to a halt in front of him. This was ridiculous! What was she thinking of? 'Look, Guy, this dress—' She lifted the diaphanous skirt, subtly shadow-printed in shades of blue, and unconsciously ran her other hand over the figure-hugging bodice. 'Well, it's fabulous. But quite frankly—'

'Quite frankly?' he pressed, his silver-grey eyes dancing with amusement.

'It must have cost a fortune and, well, I'll never wear it again, will I?' she said, trying reason on him.

'I don't see why not,' he argued. 'It's perfectly lovely.'

Kate's striking green eyes narrowed to dangerous slits of emerald light. 'That's exactly my point.'

Guy's face adopted a mildly bemused expression. 'You don't like it because it's lovely?' he queried, sliding one strong tanned hand into the pocket of his grey tailored trousers.

Conscious that her eyes had followed his every move and he'd probably noticed, Kate shifted position uncomfortably. In the process she almost toppled off the high-heeled Jimmy Choos, forcing Guy to reach out and steady her. As he stood back again she protested, 'That's exactly my point. I don't live your kind of life. I'm more of a—'

'*Garçon manqué?*' he supplied. 'Tomboy, I believe, is how you say it in English.'

'You know very well how we say everything in English,' Kate scolded, noticing how he lifted his hand and kept the back of it across his mouth so that she had no idea if he was laughing or not. 'Well, I'm hardly the Countess de Villeneuve, am I?' The words flew out of her mouth.

'Indeed. But surely it won't hurt you to wear this lovely dress for one day?'

'But if I'm clearing the cottage—'

'True,' he agreed solemnly. 'I'll have a selection of dungarees and work-boots delivered to you later this afternoon.'

Kate narrowed her eyes as she looked up at him. It was hard to tell if he was serious or joking.

'Meanwhile,' he said, 'we'll have lunch…here,' he added, pointing to the lakeside, where she could see a table had been laid with all the finest china and glass and a taupe canvas parasol had been erected to protect them from the midday sun.

'I should be getting back.'

'You will eat something first,' he said firmly, offering her his arm.

Slipping her hand through the crook of Guy's arm was like putting a key into the gate to paradise, Kate warned herself. But surely there was no harm in sampling the role for which he had dressed her, just for lunch. There was something almost unbearably seductive about strolling with a devastatingly handsome French count through an avenue of sculpted box to a winding path that led down to the edge of a crystalline lake in front of his château. And, just in case her imagination faltered, the glade in which their table was set was shielded by a group of willow trees in their first flush of greenery. They provided a whispering chorus as the light breeze danced through their supple branches and, in front of these, streamers of skylarks offered a scintillating cabaret as they dive-bombed the water to drink.

'*Mademoiselle,*' Guy murmured, releasing her arm. And then a manservant, so still, so discreet Kate hadn't even noticed him standing there, stepped forward to hold out her chair, then pour the wine and serve the salad. Guy was doing everything he could think of to help her get over the shock of the fire, she realised.

'I could get used to this,' Kate confessed as the man faded into the background again.

As Guy's sensuous lips pressed together he hummed a sound she failed to interpret.

'But, Guy, I must insist—'

'You must?' he murmured, making it sound like a challenge as he gazed at her over the rim of his wine glass.

Trying to ignore the heat that sped to the area currently enclosed by the tiniest lace thong she had ever seen in her life, Kate steeled herself to continue. 'I cannot possibly wear any of those clothes I found in the dressing room. They are far too—'

'What? Beautiful? Feminine? Tell me,' he demanded, still in the same low and very disturbing voice.

'They are all very beautiful and extremely feminine,' Kate admitted, 'but that's not what concerns me.'

Twin furrows appeared between his sweeping sable brows. 'So, what does concern you?' he pressed.

'I only needed one outfit at most,' Kate explained. 'But you must have ordered half a summer collection.'

'All of it,' he said casually. 'And the fashion house was good enough to track down shoes, bags and lingerie for me too—and at such short notice. Of course, I haven't had a chance to examine every item. So, you must choose, Kate. Keep whatever you want and I'll send the rest back. Keep everything, or nothing. It's up to you, Kate.'

Kate was far too stunned to come up with a reasoned argument. 'But I can't possibly—'

'OK, so now I've got an even better idea,' Guy said decisively.

Kate's sigh of relief was audible as she laid down her knife and fork.

'You always did like dressing up. I remember you coming to your aunt's in that hideous school uniform and then *pouf!* The next day you would reappear in some exotic concoction she had dreamed up for you. One day you were stiff and anxious and the next...'

As he paused to view her thoughtfully, as if searching for a way to describe how she had looked back then, Kate found her own concerns centring on her current appearance. Making a discreet check, she discovered just how diaphanous the top of her new dress really was.

'And the next?' she pressed, hoping to deflect Guy's interest, which she saw she had drawn to the generous amount of cleavage currently overflowing the cunningly designed bodice.

'And the next day you would be anyone you wanted to be,' he said, relaxing back with an open-armed shrug. 'Bandanna and jeans meant I had to beware of the pirate queen. Those pretty muslin skirts much like the one you wore yesterday...' He thought for a moment. 'Maybe you would be a romantic peasant girl for the day, or maybe even a fairy princess.'

'Yuk!' Kate grimaced and then looked down at the dress she was wearing. 'And this?'

Guy shrugged as he threw back his head to give a short, very masculine laugh. 'The Countess de Villeneuve, perhaps? For the day at least,' he qualified provocatively. His stare was like a challenge to which she responded exactly as he anticipated.

'I'm warning you, Guy. Don't tease me.' Kate waited for a moment until she was sure she was ready to return to the attack. 'Why don't we get back to this idea of yours?'

'Leave the clothes here,' Guy suggested casually. 'That way, any time you feel like some role play—' His brows rose infinitesimally, but enough, and there was laughter in his eyes and something darker and far more disturbing. Some of the underwear was—Kate didn't even dare think about it, at least not while she was sitting so close to him.

'Are you ready to go to the cottage now?' he said when they had finished lunch.

Kate agreed that she was. She had realised instantly that she wasn't up to sexual jousts with Guy, even if they were only verbal. Her arena was business, and if she'd had any sense that was where she would have kept their relationship. 'Yes, I'm ready,' she confirmed. 'And if the cottage has been pronounced safe—if the bedrooms are in any way habitable—I should like to stay on there. I know there will be a lot of clearing up to do before the builders and decorators can start their work and I'd like to help.' She watched his jaw tighten but, like her, Guy was intent on keeping his thoughts to himself. The most he permitted himself now was a brief nod of agreement.

'If that's what you want,' he agreed, 'Madame Duplessis will send hampers of food and drink and I'm sure we have some oil lamps and an old oil heater sómewhere that will do for now.'

'There's really no need to bother. I'll be fine,' Kate said, knowing what she really needed was a clean break with the château. Her body told her that anything other than the most limited contact with Guy, Count of Villeneuve was going to lead to complications she would never be ready to handle.

'Nonsense!' he said, springing up before she could think of any more excuses. 'I'm going to take you back there now and find out exactly what you need.'

## CHAPTER FOUR

THE drive back to the cottage took just a few minutes in one of the estate's four-wheel drive vehicles, but it was a few moments more before Kate could bring herself to check out the damage.

'Come on,' Guy urged impatiently, slamming his door. Flinging her door open, he stood there waiting. Only then did Kate's mind click into gear. He'd been up half the night on her behalf and he was sure to have other things to do. 'I'm sorry,' she said, making light of her shock at seeing the smoke-blackened exterior. 'I was just steeling myself.'

As soon as he was sure she was following, Guy strode briskly up the path. 'I wouldn't have brought you up here if the cottage was burned beyond redemption,' he called over his shoulder. Reaching the front door, he pushed it open. The first thing that hit Kate was the smell, a dank, rancid stench that caught in the back of her throat as she adjusted her eyes to the gloom.

'Look, it's not too bad,' Guy said as he forced the door across a heap of something damp that squelched as they walked over it. 'And we've had the "all clear" from the fire service and... What?' he said when she made a small wounded sound.

Maybe it didn't look too bad to him, but as far as Kate was concerned it was the end of an era and there wasn't even time to mourn. And with the deadline she had to meet the devastation inside the cottage was nothing short of a total disaster.

The flimsier objects as well as the soft furnishings had been utterly consumed, and the heavy cupboard doors as well as the beautiful oak table and rustic-style benches appeared scorched beyond redemption; the wood charred to dust in some places. But it was far more than the loss of a deadline Kate saw as she looked around. It was the loss of a very important part of her life. Shattered ornaments lay scattered about the floor, and there was no sign at all of the photograph albums she had been studying amongst the stinking wet debris. Of the two old carver chairs, one slumped miserably on three legs instead of four and the ceiling had fallen down in the far corner of the room, exposing the rafters above, though they seemed unharmed, Kate saw thankfully. But the white walls had been transformed into an ugly mishmash of yellows and browns shaded with banners of soot. A groan escaped her as she forced herself to turn full circle.

'*Arrêtes!*' Guy insisted, taking her upper arms in a strong grip as if to shake some sense into her. 'There's nothing here that my men can't repair. It's all superficial.'

As his touch ripped through her, she burst out, 'Superficial!' Kate shook her head incredulously. 'I can't believe you just said that, Guy de Villeneuve. You're such a man!'

'I certainly hope so—'

As their eyes met, the furious look she flashed at him ricocheted back on her senses. 'Only a man could look at a home reduced to a cinder and insist that the damage is superficial,' she said, shifting the heat into her accusation.

'But it is,' Guy insisted. 'The structure's sound.'

'But everything's lost!'

'Ah,' he murmured, releasing her to slip his hand into his pocket. 'Not quite everything.'

'My locket!' Kate gasped.

'The men brought it to me this morning,' he revealed, holding it so that the chain was wrapped around his wrist and the locket swung free in front of her face.

But Kate's mind was still over-loaded with emotion and for a few seconds she couldn't think straight.

'Aren't you going to say thank you?' Guy said as he took hold of her arms.

'You kept it from me,' Kate said irrationally, trying to pull away.

Guy's voice was low and intense as he stared into her eyes to deliver the correction. 'I chose my moment to give it to you. Didn't you think I would know how distressed you would be when you saw this—?' He gave a brief glance around. 'I wanted the recovery of the locket to put this calamity in perspective...make it seem what it is— superficial.'

'OK,' Kate mumbled, facing away as she struggled to untangle the jangling impressions in her head.

'That's not good enough,' Guy insisted, cupping her chin in his hand and bringing her round to face him again. 'And I'm still waiting,' he said, directing his words at eyes tightly shut.

'For?' Risking a glance at his face, Kate instantly wished she hadn't.

'For you to say thank you,' Guy murmured in a voice that made her breathing seem noisy by comparison.

Their frozen tableau of clean, neatly pressed normality should have formed an oasis amidst all the devastation, but Kate felt as if she was standing at the gateway of another world...a world she wasn't sure she should enter. It hadn't always been easy standing on the outside looking in, but it was safe.

Silence wound around them like a shield, protecting her against the reality that would have to be faced some time, but not yet, whilst ribbons of sunlight slipped through the damaged shutters to light up their faces. 'Thank you,' she murmured, dipping her head with relief that it had been safely said.

But as Guy released the chain into her hand he slipped a hand either side of her face. 'Better now?' he murmured. And this time there was no escape from his eyes. As Kate looked into them she knew that if this was another of his games it was one she hadn't played before. Her heart stopped as she saw his intention reflected in his fast darkening stare and in the curve of his sensuous mouth. But then he let her go and stood back as if to show that she was free to move, free to pretend the moment had never happened.

Then of its own accord her body inclined towards him and his mouth brushed hers with the lightest touch—a reassurance maybe, support in a difficult moment, a gesture of friendship. She didn't mean to sigh her encouragement, to move closer until his tongue teased the seam of her mouth, parting her lips, tasting, touching and exploring in the lightest most leisurely dance of retreat and advance. Her breathing raced as she felt her lips swell in response to the languorous teasing and the nip of his teeth. But he made no move to address the ache between her thighs and only went on tormenting her with the same unflinching control so that each time she tried to close the short distance between them he moved away, always denying her the firmer touch she craved.

'Stop... Stop it now, Guy!' She managed to force out at last as she stumbled away from him. 'I don't know what game you're playing but whatever it is I'm not ready for it.'

'Really?' he murmured sardonically.

'You know what I mean,' she said, covering her mouth with the back of her hand, as if that was all it took to hide her arousal. But from the look on his face the moment had passed—she might even have imagined it to judge from the steely determination on his face. But what was his game? Was this a test? If so, it seemed his intention was to prove to her that in spite of all her denials she was as attracted to him as ever. And the way he had closed himself off now from her was simply to make the point that she should not think, even for one moment, that he felt the same.

'This might look bad,' he said coolly, turning his attention to the ruined kitchen. 'But upstairs there's hardly any damage at all. And even this is all cosmetic.'

Kate's mind was still churning as she fixed her gaze on Guy's broad, uncompromising back. He was so focused, so composed. How could that be when his kiss had left her reeling and confused? And did he really expect her to be able to enter into a rational discussion about the state of the kitchen?

'Look at this, for example,' he continued, apparently unaware of her state of mind as he pointed to a row of cupboards. 'These doors can easily be replaced and they're so solid—' He rapped one with his fist and opened it. 'Everything inside is completely unharmed. 'See,' he said, whipping out a couple of terracotta bowls. 'Not even a crack in one of these. You could easily serve up a meal for half the village.'

'All of them, I hope,' Kate murmured, determined to show she could be as untroubled as he was by The Kiss.

'Ah, yes,' Guy said as he replaced the bowls. 'Your house-warming party in three weeks' time.' Planting his hands on his lean hips, he looked at her. 'I guess that's my target for getting everything here back to normal for you.'

He was clearly pleased to see what he must have imagined was her return to clear thinking, Kate thought, imposing a smile on her strained features. Lucky for her he couldn't sense the mayhem in her mind. Suddenly it was all too much for her—the loss of Aunt Alice, the deception, the devastation at the cottage, not to mention Guy's reminder of the impossible deadline she had set herself. She had to get out of the cottage—into the fresh air.

'You can cook?' Guy demanded, oblivious to the storm clouds brewing as he followed her out. 'If not, don't worry about it. I'll arrange something with Madame Duplessis. No one need ever know.'

That suggestion doused the aftershock of his kiss more

effectively than any bucket of cold water. As a child, her life had been ordered for her, but things were very different now. She was in charge of her own life. 'I can manage, thank you,' Kate broke in, turning her face to the sun as she gulped in air. Perhaps it did sound ungrateful, but she had to put him straight.

'I'm sure you can,' he said. 'But if you need any help, don't be afraid to ask.'

She couldn't let him go on. 'When I knew my career as a dancer was over...'

He broke in, taking hold of her arm for emphasis. 'I noticed your limp. You don't have to talk about it if you don't want to.'

'I retrained as a Cordon Bleu cook,' Kate went on steadily in an attempt to avoid discussing something that could only strengthen his impression of her as being the same headstrong character he had known years before.

'I'm impressed,' Guy said with a small shrug. 'But I'm more concerned about the tragic loss of your dancing career. That must have been terrible for you.'

'Not as terrible as what happened to your father...and Aunt Alice,' Kate pointed out. 'Compared to that, it hardly seems worth mentioning.'

'Of course it's worth mentioning,' Guy insisted calmly. 'You must have been at the peak of your career when it happened. I used to read about you all the time in the arts columns...and then nothing.'

Kate's mouth twisted in a wry smile. 'That's right. But I was too tall.'

'Nonsense,' Guy argued. 'All the critics said you were a dream.'

'Yes,' Kate said, forcing out a short laugh. 'But it was always my mother's dream, not mine. And in a strange sort of way the accident freed me.'

'Freed you?' he said in a puzzled voice.

'Yes. To be myself,' Kate explained. 'To do what I wanted to do.'

'To start up in business?'

He clearly found the idea bewildering, but for Kate breaking into the world of commerce had fulfilled her dreams however crazy that might seem to Guy. 'That's right,' she confirmed. 'At first I thought of becoming a chef, but that wasn't quite right for me. Then one day when I was trawling the Internet to find a holiday I hit on the idea of opening a travel agency with a difference. A one-stop shop which you could access via the Internet, put a package together yourself, but also with the option to ask for advice from staff who really knew what they were talking about. At first I was the only staff member,' she said with a self-deprecating laugh. 'But if there was one thing my career as a dancer had given me it was the chance to see the world. So Freedom Holidays took off like a rocket—beyond all my wildest expectations. At last I'd found something I wanted to do—something I enjoyed.'

'Past tense,' Guy observed shrewdly.

'Not at all,' Kate returned quickly. 'I still love what I do. But now it's time to expand.'

'And expansion doesn't always mean getting bigger,' he reasoned out loud. 'Sometimes it means taking a broader view.'

'Exactly,' she agreed, enthusing at his quicksilver grasp of the situation.

'So, what is your plan?' he said, surprising her with the accuracy and speed of his lunge into the soft, exposed heart of her deception.

'I thought you wanted to hear about what happened to me, not my business,' Kate parried. She never talked about the accident, but right now it seemed the safer…no, the only option. She saw his gaze soften fractionally.

'*Continues*, Kate.'

'It was stupid really…' Now it had come to it, she knew

it sounded nothing less than lunatic. 'I accepted a dare…'
She stopped. His face had adopted an all too familiar look.
'It was my twentieth birthday. I know.' She said it for him.
'You're thinking I should have grown out of my daredevil
phase long before then.'

Guy managed to confine himself to a wry shrug as he
waited for her to go on.

'There was a gantry over the flies,' she explained, referring to the iron structure that spanned the space high over
the backstage area in the theatre where she had been working.

'And the dare was?' he pressed when she hesitated.

'To walk across it *à pointe*.' She could only wait a few
moments when his imagination took flight and he groaned.
There really was no way to explain what she had been
doing all that way off the ground, tiptoeing across a six-
inch beam in a pair of ballet shoes. 'My fall was broken
by the ropes and—'

Guy's face tightened with concern as he held up his
hands to stop her. 'It sounds like the most horrendous accident. It's a miracle you weren't killed.'

'I know,' she said softly.

'Well, now you've returned here to Villeneuve, I hope
you can assure me that your days of risk-taking are well
and truly over.'

How was she supposed to answer that? Kate thought, as
her mind drifted back to his kiss. How did that rank on a
risk scale from one to ten? However cool Guy might be
choosing to play it now, safe men didn't kiss like that—
and cautious girls didn't let them. 'It's not always obvious
at the time that you are taking a risk,' she argued sensibly.

'It is to me,' he said vehemently. 'And now that's out
of the way,' he said, as if her compliance was a given, 'I
want to take another look at the damage so I know just who
to send round to put it right.'

*    *    *

Guy had been as good as his word, Kate thought as she stood outside the cottage watching the decorator putting the final touches to the wooden shutters. Guy's business interests might have taken him abroad, but the work had continued just as he had promised it would. And his absence had allowed Kate to concentrate on her own plans, rather than waste time on dreaming up fanciful possibilities between them—even if that didn't stop her from gazing down the lane umpteen times a day—just as she was doing now, she realised, pulling herself together.

She walked briskly back up the path to attach the last tie to the vigorous rambling rose she had managed to rescue. Now it was securely fastened around the newly painted front door it was already showing brand new clusters of hectic pink blooms after its violent upheaval. She had placed two large terracotta pots on either side of the door, each containing a miniature palm whose delicate fronds whispered a sibilant tune as the light summer breeze played through them. And the path had been repaired and then edged with every fragrant species of plant she could lay her hands on.

Standing back, Kate gave a sigh of satisfaction. On the outside, at least, she was satisfied that La Petite Maison looked as welcoming as it possibly could. But now it was time to clean her fingernails and move indoors, where the real work still had to be done. She felt a rush of excitement as she remembered that there was just a little over a week to go before her first guests arrived. And it was only a week to the famous house-warming party.

Guy had sent a brief handwritten note apologising for the fact that he was unable to give any indication as to whether he would make it back in time. But there was no risk if he did attend, Kate consoled herself. As far as Guy de Villeneuve was concerned, the many improvements to the cottage had been made for her benefit alone. And the party for the village was just what it seemed to be—a

chance for her to get to know everyone a little better. And
it was a fact that she would need to integrate herself fully
in village life if everyone was to reap the full benefit from
her new business venture.

Pushing open the front door, Kate kicked off her flip-
flops and relished the fresh clean smell. It was hard to imagine that this was the same place Guy had brought her to
after the fire. And now that she was able to look at things
calmly and objectively, she could see that the damage had
given her the chance to make some real improvements.
Once she had taken him into her confidence the builder had
come up with some of his own ideas. Knocking down the
wall between the kitchen and the morning room, for instance, had given her at least three times the space. And
when he had installed the island unit with a cooking hob
where she intended to hold some of her demonstrations, he
had suggested the addition of a part-mirrored wall behind
the other work-surfaces, allowing food preparation to be
seen clearly.

The mirrors had the added advantage of reflecting the
light, so that what had once been a cosy but decidedly
shady area had been transformed into a spacious, airy room
with plenty of natural light. To this Kate had added a number of comfortable chairs in mellow wood made snug with
plump cushions in her chosen colours of egg-yolk yellow,
white and blue. Lined white voile curtains billowed out
from the open windows and on the freshly scrubbed floor
she had placed a huge new rug in neutral shades to soften
the appearance of the original stonework. It only remained
to unpack all the equipment she had ordered and the kitchen
was ready.

'I've got the old range going for you.'

Turning to thank the builder who had made it a matter
of pride to see that she would be as comfortable as possible
as quickly as possible, Kate returned his smile of achievement. Husband of the affable lady owner of the local *fruit-*

*erie*, Giles Dumas was a walking advertisement for good diet and the outdoor life. His healthy complexion frosted with silver stubble housed a clear topaz gaze that seemed to see beyond his latest achievement and on to the next task. 'I can't thank you enough,' Kate told him.

'The bathroom's next,' he murmured, confirming her supposition that he was already planning his next job.

Giles had made sure that she had water, even if the electricity supply was proving more of a problem. But the old range was most important of all. It would heat the water and provide cooking facilities until the mains supplies could be connected. As yet there was no sign of this happening, a matter that had been referred back to the Villeneuve estate office to sort out.

'Monsieur le Comte is your friend?' Giles said as he rolled down the sleeves of his red and white checked shirt and rebuttoned the cuffs.

'That is correct,' Kate said, wondering where this was leading.

As Giles settled his omnipresent black beret to a more secure position on the crown of his head he beetled a look at her. 'Monsieur le Comte will speak to the authorities on your behalf when he returns and then you will have electricity.'

Kate smiled at his blind faith. 'I'm sure you're right, Giles. But I'm quite capable of doing that myself. And I have no idea when Monsieur le Comte is returning.'

'Allow me to put you out of your misery.'

'Guy!' Kate exclaimed accusingly. 'You startled me!' But the sight of him, darkly tanned in a casual linen suit over a simple white T-shirt, striding in through the open doorway was enough to make anyone jump, she reassured herself, swallowing deeply.

'My word, Giles,' he said, clapping the builder on the back. 'What a transformation!' Then, turning to Kate, he executed a mock-bow. 'Allow me to apologise for the in-

trusion, *mademoiselle*. And for causing you to jump, however elegantly, into the air.' But then he spoiled it all by
adding sardonically, 'I haven't known you so timid before,
Kate—or so feminine,' he finished, looking her up
and down.

Kate could see he was clearly in the mood for tormenting
her. His gaze lingered on her working uniform of bare feet,
flower-sprigged cotton skirt from the village store and the
same white blouse that had let her down once before.

'I would have changed if I had known you were coming,'
she said acerbically.

'*Mais non.* I like it,' he declared with a touch too much
relish. 'I can see La Petite Maison is bringing out the best
in you.'

Did he mean dishevelled and decidedly grubby while she
toiled at what he clearly considered were suitable tasks?
Kate's lips tightened as she squared her shoulders. 'Don't
go there, mister—'

Now it was Giles's turn to jump with alarm. Clearly
embarrassed at finding himself between his Count and a
disrespectful maiden, the elderly builder, having snatched
his beret off his head, was attempting to back his way out
of the room.

In a trice, Kate was standing between him and the door.
'No, Giles, I must insist that you share a glass of lemonade
with us. It's freshly made,' she added, fluttering around him
in decidedly un-Kate-like mode as she tried appealing to
the older man's chivalrous inclinations.

'Well, if you insist,' he said hesitantly, gazing anxiously
at Guy and then back again to Kate.

'Of course she insists. We both do,' Guy said, putting
an arm around Giles's shoulders as he led him to one of
the well-upholstered benches. 'You'll share a glass with
me, won't you? And then you can fill me in on all the latest
gossip,' he insisted with a wink to Giles, sparing a look of
amused triumph for Kate.

Kate's hands were trembling when she reached for the pitcher of juice she had left cooling in the shady depths of the vast porcelain sink. It would be nice to pretend it was righteous indignation at the way Guy always assumed control that gave her the shakes, but she knew his arrival was all it took to set her trembling. Already his presence seemed to pervade every atom of the home she was trying to build for herself. She might be tough and shrewd in business, but in business there wasn't this degree of emotion to contend with, she realised as she reached for the tumblers.

'Let me help you.'

She hadn't even realised Guy was right behind her until she heard his voice. Turning, she saw Giles comfortably ensconced on the bench where Guy had been sitting, whilst Guy had picked up one of her new beech trays.

'I'll serve,' he offered, nodding towards the heavy jug she had balanced on the side of the sink. 'That looks heavy. Let me take it.'

'I can manage.'

'You don't have to manage when I'm here,' he pointed out. 'Come on, Kate,' he murmured in her ear. 'Don't make a scene. Why should we make Giles feel uncomfortable? Give me the jug.'

Loading the tray as he asked, Kate made a detour to the old meat safe she had pressed into service until the electricity was restored before following him back to the table.

Guy had already poured the lemonade and she watched Giles begin to gulp it down. She knew he would drink quickly. He was clearly eager to be anywhere but where he found himself right now. But as Guy relaxed back against the table to take his first sip, Giles stopped drinking and stared at the glass in astonishment.

'This is delicious, *mademoiselle*.'

And then Guy's eyes flamed with approval too. 'This is seriously good, Kate,' he murmured.

'Well, don't sound too surprised,' she murmured to Guy,

raising her brows in gentle reproof. But all the same she took real pleasure watching the two men enjoying the drink she had prepared. 'Try a few of these to go with the lemonade,' she suggested, pushing the bowls and plates she had brought from the old-fashioned cooler across the table. 'Tell me what you think. And be honest. They're a trial run for the house-warming party.'

Both looked equally impressed as they surveyed the rainbow selection of sauces and neatly prepared salad vegetables.

'*Absolument delicieux,*' Guy declared after he had tried a few and exchanged several glances of appreciation with Giles.

'I'm sorry I can't offer you anything more,' Kate told them. 'But I had no means of cooking until Giles fixed the solid fuel range…'

'What else needs to be done now, Giles?' Guy cut in.

Giles continued to tuck in as he spoke. 'Nothing major on the building front, Monsieur le Comte. But the electricity is still not connected…'

'Not connected!' Guy exclaimed. 'How can that be? I left instructions before I went away that the reconnection of all the main services here was to be a priority. Why didn't you say something, Kate? How on earth have you been managing?'

'I've managed just fine, thank you.'

'But I don't understand. How could you?'

'With your oil fire and lots of candles,' she said, reminding him of the offer he had made and that Madame Duplessis had thoughtfully ensured was carried through.

'But before I went away I told my estate office to inform the authorities that La Petite Maison was being lived in once more.'

Did he mean the same secretary who had tried to prevent her from seeing Guy in the first place? Kate wondered.

'Don't worry,' she insisted. 'I shall take up the matter my-self. I'm sure it's only a question of time…'

'But you do not have much time, *mademoiselle*,' Giles exclaimed, immediately looking contrite when he realised that he had nearly let the cat out of the bag now he was sworn to secrecy over her plans for the guest house.

Instantly Kate felt guilty for having embroiled him in her plans too—plans that were rapidly getting out of hand. Laying her palm across his gnarled fist, she hurried to re-assure him. 'There's really no need for either of you to be concerned. It's something that I can take up myself now that the worst of the damage has been put to rights.'

'But Monsieur le Comte can make things happen,' Giles protested anxiously.

'So can I. So can I, Giles,' Kate told him firmly.

'Well as soon as Monsieur le Comte arranges for your electricity to be reconnected,' Giles said, clearly unconvin-ced that anyone could make things happen with quite the same speed as the Count de Villeneuve, 'I will be back to help you again.'

'I appreciate that more than I can say, Giles,' Kate said, standing as Giles prepared to leave.

'That was the best lemonade I have ever tasted, *made-moiselle*,' he said, putting his glass down on the kitchen table. 'And the dips, the *crudités* too—delicious! I shall be sure to tell Elise, my wife. We are already looking forward to your party, but now—' He rolled his eyes in a great show of anticipation.

'It looks as if I was rather presumptuous in offering you the services of my chef,' Guy remarked once Kate had seen Giles out.

'No, no,' Kate said. 'It was kind of you to offer.' Gathering her thoughts for a moment, she leaned back against the door. Even though she had been the owner of La Petite Maison for six months she had occupied the cot-tage for such a short while, yet it had been long enough for Guy to turn her whole world upside down. And the worst of it was that she prided herself on her integrity above everything. In all her business dealings her word was her bond—yet here she was holding so much back.

'What's this, Kate?'

She made a small interrogative sound as she looked at Guy and, following his gaze, she felt her stomach lurch. She should have known it would only be a matter of time before he began to tease out all the loose threads of her deception. He was standing in front of the mirrors Giles had installed for her. 'They are for...'

'*Oui?*' he pressed. 'What is this—the house of mirrors?'

'They reflect the light,' she pointed out lamely, hoping that would deflect his interest.

Guy's scepticism showed in the way his lips quirked down at the corners, but he made no comment until he turned to survey the impressive new cooking station in the centre of the room. 'Well, I must say you're well equipped,' he observed mildly. 'And this is a massive kitchen now...for someone living on their own.'

'I plan to entertain a lot,' Kate said quickly.

'That doesn't surprise me,' Guy said as he wandered across to take his pick from the plate of appetisers. 'From what I've tasted so far, an invitation to La Petite Maison is guaranteed to be the hottest ticket in town.'

'I certainly hope so,' Kate said, remembering the pleasing number of forward bookings she had already received for the cottage in its latest guise as a guest house.

'But mirrors round three sides of the room?' Guy said curiously. 'Isn't that a little excessive? You're not thinking of opening a bordello, are you?'

Kate's cheeks flamed as quite suddenly the mirrors took on a whole new range of possibilities. 'Certainly not,' she said. 'I'm fond of light, that's all.'

'If you say so.'

'I do say so.'

A few moments passed between them before Guy broke eye contact. Then, reaching inside his jacket, he extracted an envelope from the pocket.

'What's this?' Kate asked as he held it out to her.

'A copy of the restrictive covenants presently in force on La Petite Maison,' he said evenly. 'I thought you should have a look at them as it may be some time before you are able to arrange an appointment with your solicitor.'

'I'll take a good look at them,' she promised, making no move to open the envelope.

'I think you should,' Guy said as he walked to the door. 'I'd better go. I've been away from things long enough.' He paused with his hand on the door handle. 'We'll have a chat about those covenants over dinner some time.'

Kate managed a tense nod. Her fingers were burning with the urge to rip open the package and see just what new problems stood in her way. Guy would never have wasted a visit for no reason. Whatever information was contained within the documents was sure to be dynamite. His expression now was impenetrable and she didn't flatter herself that he had come round for a replay of The Kiss. In fact, since that moment he hadn't betrayed by so much as a glance or a smile that he had kissed her in so skilful, so knowing a way—while Kate wondered, on the other hand, if she would ever be able to put it out of her mind.

As Guy strode off down the path Kate's grip on the envelope tightened. Seeing him swing into the driver's seat, she looked around the room, trying to see the kitchen through his eyes. Had he guessed what she intended to do? Had he been convinced by her explanation that she loved cooking…loved to share her passion with friends? Whatever he thought he would find out the truth soon enough.

Somewhere just beyond the tousled hedge she heard the engine roar into life, bringing on another rush of guilt. She swallowed it back fast. There was nothing between them.

Even The Kiss had meant nothing to him. He had just slipped back into the habit of a lifetime—teasing her as he always had—except that she wasn't a child any longer. Impatient with herself for dwelling on a hopeless situation, Kate turned her attention to those things she could do something about.

By the time she reached the long oak table she already had the documents out of the envelope. Business was her anchor, a forum in which she excelled and, most crucially, an arena where emotions played no part. A sense of relief swept over her as she sat down. But she could only bring herself to skim the top sheet. However hard she struggled to keep her mind on the task and her eyes firmly focused on the page, all she could think of was Guy.

# CHAPTER FIVE

'MEGAN! I can't believe it's you!' Enveloped in a hug that went the best part to smothering her, Kate clung to Aunt Alice's friend as if she would never let her go.

'There now, stand back and let me look at you for a minute, will you?' the older woman insisted. 'Tears? What's this, pet?'

'Surprise at seeing you,' Kate lied as she dashed them away. Tears were completely out of character, but since returning to France everything seemed to have gone haywire. And now she was so pathetically grateful to see Megan O'Reilly, who was to be Course Leader for the art groups Kate planned to host, it was ridiculous. It was a thrill just to hear the lilt of her Irish accent again and such a relief not to be alone in the venture any longer. Pulling herself together, Kate began, 'Megan, you look...'

'As disreputable as ever, I know,' Megan said dismissively. 'Kettle on?' she added hopefully, looking past Kate into the kitchen as she heaved the bulging carpet bag at her feet back on to her ample shoulder.

'I'm sorry,' Kate said as she took in the state of Megan's colourful multi-layered clothing. 'It's so hot today. You must be exhausted. Come on in.'

'My, my... You've made quite a few changes since your aunt Alice lived here,' Megan observed as she looked around the room. 'And all these mirrors—what've you got planned, Kate? Something naughty, I hope?'

'I thought they'd be useful for teaching—help people see what I'm doing during demonstrations,' Kate explained. 'You're the second person to remark on them,' she admitted, smiling to herself as she put the kettle on the hob.

'How is his lordship?'

'How did you know I meant Guy?'

'Oh, come now, Kate,' Megan said as she eased her bare feet out of a pair of shabby loafers and wiggled her toes. 'There's no need to be coy with me. Don't tell me you two haven't been catching up on old times?'

'I don't know what you mean,' Kate said, glad to have her back turned as she buried her head in a cupboard to search out some crockery.

'I might be an old fogey,' Megan remarked dryly, 'but I can still remember the sparks flying between you two when you used to come here as a youngster. I can't believe he's ignoring you now you're here for good...'

'Ah—'

'You haven't told him!'

'Not exactly,' Kate admitted, spooning coffee granules into the mugs.

'Don't you think it's about time you did?' Megan demanded as she replanted the chopsticks holding up her cloud of magenta hair.

'It's not that easy, Megan.'

'Don't be silly. Of course it's that easy,' Megan argued, bustling over to the range to assume control of the coffee preparation. 'Go and sit down and tell me what's been happening. I know something's up—and if we're going to be working together...'

'You're right,' Kate said, going to perch on a stool. 'It's only fair to tell you that this latest business venture of mine probably won't even get off the ground.'

'What?' Megan said, throwing a stare over her shoulder. 'I can see I got here in the nick of time. This is more serious than I thought. Here,' she said, advancing towards Kate like a galleon in full sail. 'Drink your coffee and then you'd better start right back at the beginning and tell me what I've missed.'

'But you've seen enough contracts in your time,' Megan

remarked when Kate had brought her up to speed. 'How different can this one be?'

'Strictly speaking it isn't a contract, it's a list of covenants,' Kate explained. 'Secondly, the only document I've read so far is a translation—'

'And the original is where?' Megan said between bites of her third slice of lemon drizzle cake.

'With my solicitor,' Kate reassured her. 'No wonder he was desperate to speak to me…'

'But you'll ask him to obtain an independent translation?' Megan cut in.

'Already done. I telephoned him just before you arrived.'

'Good,' Megan said, pushing her plate away as if the whole matter had been put to bed. 'So while your solicitor's attending to that side of things, why don't you and I concentrate on Freedom Holidays' newest new venture, Freedom Breaks? Our first guests arrive when?'

'Too soon.'

'Well, don't sound so worried,' Megan said, patting Kate's arm with a plump, lavishly beringed hand. 'This old carpet bag of mine is like a magician's trunk.' She opened it up to illustrate her point, allowing a shambles of well-used artists' paraphernalia to spill across the floor. 'I've got everything in here to keep the world and his wife hap… Who's that now?' she said, breaking off to stare towards the door. 'Could this be our first guest?' She cocked her head to one side like a super-alert squirrel.

Kate's gaze switched desperately from Megan, to the mess on the floor, to the door. If it was Guy he wouldn't wait to be invited into the cottage, he would walk straight in as he always had… Springing to her feet, she pelted across the room, hoping to get there before he could…hoping somehow to distract him so he wouldn't notice. It never occurred to her once that it could be anyone else, and by the time she opened the door her heart was leaping around in her chest like a demented rabbit.

'Guy, what a surprise,' she lied, flinging open the door

and then closing it again quickly to just a crack. She saw his eyebrows quirk with bemusement as she tried in vain to block his view into the cottage.

'Are you busy?' he said, peering over her head. 'If so, I can always call back another time—'

'We're not too busy to see you,' Megan called out before Kate had the chance to stop her. 'There's only me here, Your Worship—'

'Now, Megan, stop that,' Guy insisted, moving past Kate to sweep Megan off her feet as if she weighed no more than a baby. 'I've told you before, Megan O'Reilly, I'm the only one licensed to tease around here—'

'Licensed to thrill, more like,' Megan declared, making a great fuss of straightening her clothes as he set her down. 'Look at you!' she said, standing back to give him a proper inspection. 'Blue jeans and work shirt! And here was me thinking that real counts walked around in powdered wigs with a flurry of flunkeys trailing after them.'

'Once upon a time, maybe,' Guy said, grinning. 'But this is here and now, Megan, when even real counts have to get down and dirty checking out the stock in their cellars.'

Megan's brows rose in twin arches of mischief. 'If you need any help with the stock-taking—'

Kate shut the door with a bang as if to shock some sanity back into Megan's thinking. She shouldn't be encouraging Guy; she should be finding some way of getting rid of him before he drew his own conclusions from the dozens of paint brushes littering the floor... But even Megan seemed dazed when presented by such an impossibly virile and aristocratic male.

'If I do need any help, Megan, you'll be the first person I call on,' Guy promised.

But, in spite of his warm assurances, Kate felt herself growing increasingly tense. His hail-fellow-well-met eye-line might be resolutely fixed on Megan's face but his lips were tugged down in an unmistakable show of speculation. And what he said next only confirmed her suspicions.

'So, what are you doing here, Megan?' he said, affecting a harmless interest. 'I thought you had settled into that teaching job at the college. The term hasn't finished already, has it?'

The silence only lasted for a moment, but for Kate it seemed to go on for ever. And when Megan did speak her voice had lost its customary brightness, leaving it dry and unconvincing. 'I had a better offer—' Her gaze glanced apologetically off Kate's.

'Really?' Guy said mildly. 'Anything exciting?'

'Ooh, yes,' she began enthusiastically. Then, remembering she wasn't supposed to talk about it, she pressed her lips flat.

'Aren't you allowed to discuss it?' Guy prompted sympathetically.

'The details aren't finalised yet,' Megan explained awkwardly, spreading her arms wide in a gesture of innocence and resignation.

Kate knew Megan had always found it impossible to tell untruths, but at least Guy didn't press her. He just stood viewing them both with his arms loosely crossed over his chest as if they were a couple of naughty schoolgirls and he their indulgent master.

'Perhaps you can enlighten me, Kate?' he said, switching his attention abruptly to her.

The suggestion was made so lightly...almost playfully, anyone else might have been taken in and been tempted to lower their guard, but it didn't fool Kate for a minute. Guy was hot on the trail. He probably only needed a few more pieces of the jigsaw and—

'So, how is her ladyship bearing up, Guy?' Megan demanded in a voice grown unusually strident.

'Well enough, I think.'

A few moments passed during which Kate was relieved to see Guy accept Megan's conversational detour.

'You don't sound too sure,' Megan observed gently, with

the familiarity years of acquaintance with Guy's family had conferred upon her.

'She's taking a long time to get over the loss of my father.'

'Of course,' Megan agreed softly. 'As you must be, Guy.'

His expression and the tilt of his head confirmed her deduction. 'And she misses Madame Broadbent too—we all do...' His gaze found Kate's and held there for a moment.

That look was the key to unlocking Kate's feelings...and her doubt too. What would Aunt Alice have made of her plans and the deception she now seemed locked into? She had to remind herself that it was for love of Aunt Alice that she found herself in Villeneuve at all. But surely Aunt Alice must have intended her to live in the cottage when she left it to her...and everything Aunt Alice stood for was encapsulated in her plans for La Petite Maison—love, sanctuary, happiness, fun and relaxation, self-fulfilment...

Dragging her eyes away from Guy, she found them drawn back to Megan. Even the little she had read about the covenants had told her that carrying out any form of business at the cottage was expressly forbidden... Forgetting the potential for financial loss, Megan had given up her job, her whole way of life, to come and teach at La Petite Maison. Kate's mouth firmed as she considered the implications. One thing was sure—she had gone too far to back out now.

'Did you come for anything special, Guy?' She forced a little steel into her voice so that the subtext suggested she had lots of things to be getting on with, as must he...

'Should I have made an appointment?' he demanded, throwing her a darkly amused glance from beneath an extraordinary fringe of pitch-black lashes.

'An appointment would have made everything possible,' Kate said innocently, just to show she hadn't forgotten their initial confrontation at the château.

'Everything?' Guy mused softly, as he sampled the stubble on his chin with a strong tanned hand. 'Now you do have my full attention.'

'Now, now,' Megan warned, coming to stand between them. 'That's enough fooling around for one day, your High and Mightyness, or it's back to the dungeons for you.'

'If you say so, Megan O'Reilly,' Guy agreed, holding up his hands in mock-submission. 'Who am I to countermand the order of a direct descendant of the illustrious Brian Boru that ancient High King of Ireland?'

Well done, Megan! Kate thought, noticing how her friend had concealed the evidence of her impending tutorials with a simple sweep of her dirndl skirt. But she should have known that it was far too little too late to fool Guy.

'That's rather a lot of paintbrushes you've dropped there, Megan. Even for you—'

Kate could only look on helplessly as he hunkered down. Pushing Megan's skirt aside, he gathered up an armful of brushes and then looked up, baiting Kate with a triumphant stare.

'Hey!' Megan exclaimed, performing an impromptu tap dance on the spot. 'Less of this rifling beneath an old woman's skirts…and watch how you handle those brushes, young Guy. I'll not have their tips mashed by you.'

Getting up, Guy handed them to her. 'I believe you dropped these, Ms O'Reilly.'

'And I'll have less of your blarney,' Megan exclaimed, clearly flustered. 'Kate and me's got things to talk about—'

'So you're not going to offer me a piece of that delicious-looking gâteau—'

'Cake,' Megan corrected, moving the plate away from him and planting herself firmly in front of it.

'Of course you can have some,' Kate said, relenting. If they sent him packing he'd only be back—and he might have come about something important—like saying he would overlook the covenants. Before she knew it he had dropped into a chair, groaning with contentment as he bit into the softly yielding lemon sponge.

'Delicious,' he murmured, closing his eyes to savour it. 'I must have more.'

'No, you mustn't,' Megan said decisively, swooping on the door and holding it open for him. 'I'll not have you shirking your duties now you're shouldering the responsibility of this estate.'

Guy took Megan's mock-scolding a lot better than she took his teasing, Kate noticed. But as he reached the door he paused. Sweeping up Megan's hand in his own, he brought it to his lips and murmured, 'I'll only do as you say if you agree to have dinner with me at the château this evening, Ms O'Reilly, and be sure to bring along your delightful hostess, Mademoiselle Foster. Then,' he added, throwing a penetrating glance at Kate, 'we can discuss the possibility of art lessons—privately, or in a group, it makes no difference to me. Though we would have to find you some accommodation where you could teach,' he pointed out while his eyes affected a beguiling innocence. 'The covenants on this cottage are quite specific, you know, Megan. And I'm sure you wouldn't want to encourage Kate to fall foul of them. Well, am I right, Ms O'Reilly?'

As he made a final mocking bow, Megan made a noise roughly similar to Concorde taking off. 'That boy doesn't change,' she complained as Kate went to shut the door on him.

'That *boy* is nearly forty years old, over six foot tall and has amassed a fortune in the region of a billion Euros,' Kate pointed out quietly as she watched Guy stride off down the path. 'He's no fool…'

'I'll expect you both at eight,' he called back, almost as if he knew she would still be there watching him.

'He's still a boy to me,' Megan grumbled, knowing she had been well and truly outmanoeuvred. 'I just hope he knows how to cook.'

'I think he keeps a chef at the château now,' Kate murmured distractedly as her eyes trailed Guy's back until he had disappeared out of sight.

'Well, you're taking it all very calmly, I must say,' Megan observed when Kate finally let the latch drop.

Leaning back against the door, Kate exhaled with relief.

'Well, say something,' Megan pressed. 'Aren't you worried at all?'

'Of course I'm worried. And not just about the covenants.'

'Explain.'

It wouldn't make Megan feel any better to know that the covenants were by far the least of Kate's worries. 'What can I do, Megan?' she said finally. 'We'll just have to carry on with our plans as if everything was OK.'

'And Guy?' Megan pressed.

'I'll tell Guy—when the moment's right.'

'And when will that be?' Megan demanded, drumming her fingertips on the table.

'Before our first guests arrive,' Kate said, more in an effort to convince herself than in an attempt to placate Megan.

'Just don't leave it until the last minute.'

'I won't,' Kate said confidently. 'Now, would you like a bath? Thanks to Giles mending the range I've got plenty of hot water, even if I'm still waiting for the electricity to be switched on.'

'No electricity!' Megan exclaimed. 'Lord save us! What are you thinking, child? You can't run a guest house without electricity...'

'I've managed perfectly well up until now,' Kate replied. 'And if necessary I shall run the cottage for profit in exactly the same way. Because you see, Megan, no one—not even Guy, Count de Villeneuve himself—is going to stop me making La Petite Maison one of the most successful retreats in the world.'

'Then I wish you luck, Kate,' Megan said, suddenly serious. 'Because if I know Guy, you're going to need it.'

*   *   *

He sent a car for them. Not just any old car, or the four-wheel-drive Guy used to get about the estate, but a sleek aubergine-coloured limousine complete with uniformed driver.

'Are you impressed? Because I am!' Megan enthused, though Kate noticed her eyes were on the driver rather than the car.

Kate hummed her agreement as she gazed out of the window. How she had ever agreed to this she had no idea. And she was wearing The Dress. She gave a wry smile. Once she would probably have turned up in blue jeans with holes in them just to be awkward, but now… Well, it was rather nice to wear a couture dress for once. In fact, now she had the money to do so, she would probably wear a lot more of them. Guy had given her an appetite—

'All right, pet? No regrets about this dinner engagement?'

'Not yet,' Kate admitted wryly.

Guy was waiting for them outside the grand double entrance door to the château. His pale jacket only accentuated the rich bronze tones of his skin and Kate thought his muscular legs seemed longer than ever as he loped down the steps to greet them.

'Welcome,' he exclaimed, holding open the door for her before the chauffeur could get to it. 'Welcome to Château Villeneuve, Kate. It's good to have you here for a social visit rather than a period of recuperation.'

'A very short recuperation,' she reminded him as his warm hand closed around hers.

'But an enjoyable one, I hope.'

'Of course. I have always loved the château,' she said, struggling to keep her voice even while he kept hold of her hand.

'Well, you will be seeing it at its best tonight. I have arranged for all the lights to be turned on when it is quite dark and that runs into tens of thousands of bulbs. It should be quite a sight,' he promised. 'And for you, Ms O'Reilly—'

he turned and, having slipped Kate's hand through his arm he offered his other to Megan '—I have invited another good friend of mine, Professor Gilman from the Tokyo Gallery in Paris, to discuss developments in modern art with you.'

'Professor Gilman!'

Kate could see that Megan was really impressed. 'That's good of you, Guy,' she said, giving his arm a squeeze.

'Good? It's bloody marvellous!' Megan exclaimed. 'Have you any idea who Professor Gilman is, Kate?'

'None. But I'm sure you'll enlighten me,' Kate teased her old friend distractedly while her mind was still fixed on corded muscles beneath an impeccably tailored suit. 'Will your mother be joining us, Guy?' she said, determined to keep her rational mind in the ascendant.

'It's too soon to tell,' he replied.

A trace of melancholy darkened the brilliance of his eyes as he turned to look at her. 'I had hoped that when she heard you were here she would come down from her room. But, well, we shall see. I shall not press her.'

'If I can do anything…anything at all.'

'I'll let you know,' he said, smiling at Megan when she expressed the same sentiments.

Following effortless introductions by Guy, Megan was soon deep in conversation with Professor Gilman, who turned out to be a shrewd-looking middle-aged woman in a designer suit rather than the hoary old man of Kate's imagination. 'You did well there,' she told Guy as they stood watching the two women stroll up the sweeping marble staircase to admire his works of art.

'I gave the ancestors leave of absence,' he explained. 'All the older paintings are being stored in the attic rooms and I've replaced them with a rather interesting collection of modern works—some of them by students I think might have a future…'

'I meant you've done well introducing Megan to Professor Gilman,' Kate said, unlinking her arm when

Guy made no move to do so. 'They seem to have a lot in common.'

'I like to bring people together,' he said simply. Then, turning to Kate, he surveyed her slowly and appreciatively, his silver-grey eyes darkening as they lingered on her face. 'Thank you for wearing that dress.'

'It's no hardship,' she admitted with more bravura than she felt. There was a chance she could melt into a puddle of desire right there in front of him when she saw what he meant to do.

Lightly, almost lazily, he ran the tip of one finger down from just beneath her cleavage to a point where the skirt flirted out around her hips. '''See where she comes, apparelled like the spring—'''

'Guy, I—'

'Bellini?'

'I thought it was Shakespeare—'

'Drink, silly.'

'Oh, yes please.' Had her wits taken flight? Kate wondered as he reclaimed her arm. Arousal threw rosy shadows across her cheeks, but she knew it was far safer to imagine it was the suggestion of champagne cocktails that put the heat into her face. As a child she had always envied the guests at the château the fragrant peach juice and champagne mix, which she remembered them sipping out of tall crystal flutes.

'Do you remember?' Guy guessed, as he drew her across the hall.

'When you made one specially for me?'

'I put a drop of champagne on the top—'

'It tickled my nose. Yes, I remember,' she said.

'I might allow you to have a slightly stronger mix tonight.'

'You'll allow?' she challenged softly.

'Doesn't the idea of being mastered appeal to you…if only for an evening?' he suggested provocatively as they walked out on to the terrace.

'Equality appeals to me far more.'

'In some things, perhaps.'

'In everything,' Kate insisted, with a little more force than she had intended, but she had to do something to marshal her wayward senses. To her surprise Guy seemed to like her answer.

'Still the same feisty Kate.'

'And does that please you?'

'*Mais oui*,' he said, throwing her a long steady look. 'It pleases me very much.'

It was hard to think straight when she was being bombarded with sensation. In spite of his reserve since The Kiss, what Guy seemed to be saying was that he wanted her. Could it be true? Everything about the setting conspired against it. There were at least three servants standing discreetly in the shadows of the terrace—and then there was Megan—and the Professor.

Kate's head shot up abruptly as Guy pressed the foaming glass into her hand. Was she going crazy? Had she lost all semblance of sanity? This wasn't a game. This was Count Guy de Villeneuve and she was Kate Foster, a successful businesswoman certainly, but one who moved in a different world from the enigmatic man by her side. Her fantasies seemed to suggest that she should simply take him by the hand and lead him upstairs to one of the twenty or so bedroom suites… She gulped the whole glass down barely tasting it. A one-night stand—was that really what she wanted? A man like Guy would think nothing of a woman who threw herself at him. Kate knew from the scandal sheets that there were more of those than he knew what to do with already. They had all met the same fate, she reminded herself, willing ice into her veins and stone into her heart.

'Why so serious, Kate?' Guy asked as he refilled her glass.

'You don't want to know.'

'Oh, but I do,' he argued as his lips tugged down in a

rueful smile. 'Perhaps this second glass will help…if you sip it.'

Kate's senses flared at the reproof. She loved it when he scolded her. It was no use pretending. Independence was fine in the real world, but this was a moment out of time where fantasies ruled. She wanted nothing more than to be taken by him into the deepest heart of his fairy-tale château; a place that was dark and still. Perhaps to the dungeons where he could tie her up with silken ropes and keep her for himself for ever…

'Dinner is served, sir.'

'Kate?'

Kate woke as if from a trance, a dangerous trance, she realised, as she felt her nipples rubbing painfully on the cleverly concealed bones as they fought the tight confines of the bodice. And as she took Guy's arm again and began to walk she realised that the deliciously sensitised place between her legs had assumed such a high state of arousal no amount of self-control could hope to purge it now. She was wet. Very, very wet. She could only be thankful that the delicate skirt of the dress was composed of several layers and all of them shaded—a damp stain wouldn't show— though it was almost impossible to hide the state she was in when her rapid breathing had to struggle to keep pace with her heart.

'Are you all right?' Guy murmured with his mouth very close to her ear.

'I'm fine—perhaps a little cold,' she added as a quiver ran through her from the crown of her head to the tips of her toes. Walking with Guy was like taking a shower of sensation, Kate thought, basking in the torturing needles as they raced each other through her body. And then, just when she had believed it impossible to feel anything more acutely, as they were about to leave the terrace and enter the château again, he held the door open for her—but, instead of standing back while she walked through, he remained with his hand leaning against it so that she was forced to pass under his arm. The sense of domination was overwhelming. With that one gesture he made her feel tiny and vulnerable and cherished, whilst he towered over her like some lusty knight from an ancient engraving; commanding and powerful, seductive and vigorous...

'Dinner will be served on the Grand Terrace,' he said as he took her through another door. 'From here you can see all the lights.'

Collecting herself, Kate turned around. What she saw was completely mesmerising. 'I've never seen anything so lovely,' she murmured. From every window in every turret of the château lights twinkled and blazed against the deep blue velvet of the cloudless night sky.

'Do you like it?'

'Like it? It's absolutely stunning—'

'But?'

'But nothing—except...'

'Yes?' he prompted as they walked towards the intimate table set for four under a silken canopy in the centre of the huge formal terrace.

'So many more people could have enjoyed it. It's such a shame your father couldn't have...' She could have bitten off her tongue when she saw the flash of pain in Guy's eyes.

'There was never any money to do this,' he said quietly as he held out her chair.

'And this is one thing on which I will not compromise,' he reminded her. 'The Villeneuve estate cannot play host to hordes of people and remain a smooth-running machine...'

'A smooth-running machine,' Kate echoed softly.

'You don't approve?'

'For a business?' She shrugged. 'Yes, of course, I like to think that my business is a smooth-running machine. But Château Villeneuve is so beautiful, Guy. The architecture, the grounds, the interior are all exquisite.'

'All the more reason, surely, to keep it exclusive, to retain its mystique, preserve its perfection.'

'You make it sound like a museum.'

'And so it is, in many ways.'

'Oh?' Kate said softly. 'I thought it was your home.'

Megan and Professor Gilman joined them then, remarking on the splendour of the lighting display as they walked up the broad expanse of stone steps that led up to the terrace.

'Everything all right, Kate?' Megan asked discreetly as she took her place at the table.

'Fine.'

'Don't lie to me,' Megan whispered.

'All right, then,' Kate said, flashing a glance at Guy, who was conferring with his sommelier on the serving of the wine, and Professor Gilman, who was studying an interesting modern silver peppershaker. 'I can tell you now that he's absolutely adamant about enforcing the no-holiday-home rule on the estate. The only way I could get away with it is to offer free holidays—make out that everyone was my personal guest…'

'Now there's a thought.'

'And where would your wages come from?'

'Point taken.'

'But look at all this, Megan,' Kate said, swivelling round in her seat. 'There's nothing like it in the whole of Europe—but at the same time there's no life here. It's fabulously beautiful, but sterile and bleak.'

'It needs an injection of Kate, if you ask me,' Megan supplied, planting her chin on her hand as she surveyed the spectacle of lights.

'The only thing missing here are the crowds,' Professor Gilman said when Guy had finished his discussion.'

'*Exactement*,' Guy said, shooting a look at Kate as if to make sure she had heard the professor's remark.

'But a few more people couldn't hurt,' Professor Gilman added, unaware of the undercurrents around the table. 'Forgive my bluntness, Count, but I can't help thinking that you must get awfully lonely here.'

'Lonely? No,' he said. 'I confess there used to be a lot more people here when there were holiday homes on the estate. But I'm afraid there just isn't room for that sort of thing now.'

'I can understand your reticence,' the Professor continued. 'I have seen some dreadfully insensitive commercialisations of similar heritage sites. But surely several discreet properties could only enhance the area—give it the appearance of a real working estate. I imagine that most of your staff live in the village these days?'

'That's true,' Guy admitted. 'But I'm sure with the right incentives I could lure them back here.'

'Surely not, when they have everything they need on their doorstep,' the Professor argued. 'Whereas one or two holiday homes of the type I've described might add a little spice to this glorious but rather secluded environment. After all, people are prepared to make a little more effort in the short term…'

'Ah, that's where Mademoiselle Foster comes in,' Guy said dryly.

'Oh, really?' the Professor said, turning to Kate. 'I had no idea that you lived here.'

'I have the only remaining holiday home on the estate.'

'Is that right?' the Professor said, her curiosity aroused.

'I believe Kate has some innovative ideas for the place,' Guy said innocently.

'Ideas?' Professor Gilman said, turning to Kate. 'For a business?'

If Professor Gilman had been anyone else Kate might have suspected Guy had put her up to it. She looked across the table to see if Megan could come up with another of her brilliant diversionary conversational tactics. But she was out of luck this time.

'Why don't you explain what you intend to do with La

Petite Maison, Kate,' Guy suggested dryly. 'I can see that you would like to hear more, Professor Gilman.'

Oh, no you don't, Kate thought, shrewdly side-stepping the trap. 'Professor Gilman, I would be delighted to send you some promotional literature,' she said calmly, 'once we are up and running.'

'I'll look forward to receiving it,' the Professor replied, giving Kate an amused, measuring look.

As the Professor prepared to leave later that evening Megan leapt up too. 'Would you mind if I shared your taxi, Professor Gilman? I fear I won't be much company. My eyes are playing up—the onset of a migraine, perhaps,' she said, looking apologetically at Kate.

'Shall I come with you?' Kate said, half standing.

'No offence, but I'd like to go straight to bed,' Megan explained, pressing her back down in the chair again. 'That sometimes gets rid of the symptoms—prevents a full-blown attack.'

'I'll call my driver at once,' Guy said.

'No, no, don't trouble,' Megan insisted. 'It's only a hop, skip and a jump back to the cottage and I'm sure Professor Gilman won't mind…'

'Of course I don't mind,' the Professor confirmed.

Guy called a member of his staff across. 'Would you take these ladies to collect their wraps?'

'I really should go with them,' Kate said, starting to get up.

Guy put his hand on her arm, stopping her. 'Please don't,' he said softly. 'My mother may yet feel strong enough to come down and…'

'I'm sorry,' Kate said, not knowing which way to turn. 'Of course I'll stay. If there's even the slightest chance…' She stopped and put her hand on top of the clenched fist he was resting on the table. 'The last few months must have been dreadful for you, Guy, assuming the responsibilities of the estate whilst you were still suffering the aftermath of such a dreadful loss.'

# Play the Lucky Hearts Game

and get...

## 2 FREE BOOKS
### and a FREE MYSTERY GIFT...

**yes!** YOURS to KEEP!

I have scratched off the silver card. Please send me my *2 FREE BOOKS* and *FREE mystery GIFT.* I understand that I am under no obligation to purchase any books as explained on the back of this card.

*Scratch Here!*

then look below to see what your cards get you... 2 Free Books & a Free Mystery Gift!

**306 HDL DU6W**　　　　　　　**106 HDL DU7E**

FIRST NAME

LAST NAME

ADDRESS

APT.#

CITY

STATE/PROV.

ZIP/POSTAL CODE

(H-P-08/03)

Twenty-one gets you
**2 FREE BOOKS**
and a *FREE MYSTERY GIFT!*

Twenty gets you
**2 FREE BOOKS!**

Nineteen gets you
**1 FREE BOOK!**

***TRY AGAIN!***

# The Harlequin Reader Service® — Here's how it works:

If offer card is missing write to: Harlequin Reader Service, 3010 Walden Ave., P.O. Box 1867, Buffalo NY 14240-1867

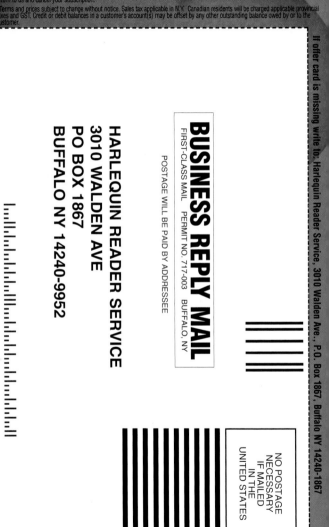

**BUSINESS REPLY MAIL**
FIRST-CLASS MAIL    PERMIT NO. 717-003    BUFFALO, NY

POSTAGE WILL BE PAID BY ADDRESSEE

HARLEQUIN READER SERVICE
3010 WALDEN AVE
PO BOX 1867
BUFFALO NY 14240-9952

NO POSTAGE
NECESSARY
IF MAILED
IN THE
UNITED STATES

Guy took a few moments to respond and then his mouth twisted in bitter agreement. 'Taking over the business was nothing, Kate. That's what I do. But losing my father...' He gave a long shuddering sigh and it was a few moments more before he could bring himself to speak. 'The accident, your aunt Alice...' He wiped a hand across his eyes as if to try and erase all the painful memories. 'It was all so dreadful,' he said in a voice that was barely audible, 'and so fast... I still can't believe he's gone.'

Reaching out, Kate put her hand on his arm as he continued to stare blindly across the terrace. 'Would it help to talk about it?'

'It won't bring my father back,' he told her bleakly. 'I loved him so much, Kate.'

'I know that,' she said softly. 'And you're still suffering from shock, Guy. It takes time to develop strategies for coping with something so terrible...so unexpected.'

He nodded agreement. 'And now my mother's health seems to be failing.'

'But maybe there's a chance that can be reversed,' Kate cut in thoughtfully.

'Do you really think so?' he said, touching her with his eagerness.

Kate pressed her lips together as she thought about it. 'She must feel lost—uncertain as to how she will carry on without your father. It must seem to her as if the whole fabric of her life has been ripped into shreds. But if she was given a new sense of purpose—of self-worth...'

'But how, Kate? How?'

'I'm not sure yet,' Kate admitted honestly. 'But if you'll let me, I'd like to try and help.'

When Professor Gilman and Megan returned they were forced to abandon the conversation. Kate didn't feel proud of herself when Professor Gilman slipped in a few more discreet enquiries regarding her future plans and she fielded them with the same aplomb that had always left her with a sense of satisfaction in the past. The reason for that was

Guy, she thought. He had always been a tower of strength, not just to her but to his family and everyone connected with him. Tonight he had revealed his most private wounds to her and they went deeper than she could ever have imagined. Without careful nursing they might never heal.

# CHAPTER SIX

'YOU must be rather pleased with yourself,' Guy observed as they waved off the Professor's taxi. 'Dodging Professor Gilman's question about what you intend to do here,' he clarified as he cupped her elbow to guide her up the steps.

Whatever her thoughts on his state of mind, this was not the time for truth games, Kate decided. Not while there was still a chance of a meeting with his mother. A bad atmosphere between them would make such a meeting impossible. 'No dodging about it,' she said, fighting to keep her mind on track while her senses were flaming at his touch. 'Good business practice, that's all. I don't expect you to tell me about your confidential dealings and until I'm ready to go public you'll just have to put up with the little you know.'

'Which is nothing,' Guy pointed out in a low drawl that strummed a quivering chord of pure sensation up and down her spine.

Kate watched as suspicion honed his keen grey gaze into a laser beam trained on her face. 'That must make quite a change for you, Guy,' she said, as uncertainty made her revert to the light banter that had always brought her close to him in the past. She wasn't expecting to be swung around quite so forcibly.

'*Ca suffit maintenant!* This is no joking matter, Kate,' he said tersely. 'I am through playing games. Those covenants stand. I forbid you to operate a business on my land.'

'You forbid?'

'You heard me,' he said firmly. 'I have already conceded the point of you retaining La Petite Maison for your own use, but I will not be pushed into agreeing to some wild scheme…'

'Wild scheme?' Kate said angrily as she attempted to shake herself free. 'I lay all my business plans with great care, or have you forgotten the success I've had already with Freedom Holidays?'

'I confess I'd forgotten what it feels like to run up against you,' Guy admitted as he tightened his grip.

Kate shivered as she noticed something very dark and dangerous brewing in his eyes.

'*Oh, pour l'amour de Dieu*, Kate! Do your worst,' he grated, holding her so close now her lips tingled in response. 'I'm ready for you.'

'Oh, really?' she challenged.

'Really. And you will do what I say,' he added with the force of inborn authority.

She should have moved then—moved as soon as she saw the expression in his eyes warning her that he was brutally aroused—and not just by the conflict between them. She knew she should struggle, but his hands were too skilful and knew her too well. Their touch was so light and seductive and she had waited so long. Holding her locked in the arrogance of his heated gaze, Guy began to feather touches across her shoulders and down her arms. He had no need to do more. She came to him willingly, eagerly, surprising them both with the force of her desire.

'No,' he murmured sternly, holding her away from him. 'Not here and not now.' And, easing her arms away from his neck, he took her by the hand and led her out into the garden again. Fountains were playing a soothing tune in hidden courtyards and the scent of lavender hung heavily in the air as he took her through an iron gate that led into a large cobbled yard in the gardeners' kingdom. He kept her close by his side as he took her down a flight of steep stone steps and Kate was forced to cling to his hand as she peered into the gloom, wondering where he was taking her. Their footsteps echoed eerily in the still black night and when they reached the bottom she couldn't resist an anxious glance back up to the top.

'Having second thoughts?' Guy suggested dryly.

'Certainly not.' But she was shivering now and not from the cold, for the air was heavy and warm, but from a heady mix of uncertainty, expectation and desire.

Guy's firm lips curved in a hard smile. 'Well, if you're quite sure...' He pushed open a heavy oak door to reveal a brilliantly lit, château-sized potting shed with a stone floor where row upon row of new young plants on tiered platforms awaited transfer to the flower beds outside. He heard her gasp and turned around. 'Not quite what you expected?' he murmured.

It certainly wasn't. With one of the most beautiful homes in Europe at his disposal it was an odd place for a romantic tryst—if that was what he intended. 'Are you sure you haven't brought me down here to lock me in and throw away the key?'

'I hadn't thought of that,' he admitted throwing her a look. 'Don't tempt me.'

As he started to walk away from her Kate couldn't stop herself blurting out, 'Don't leave me.'

'I won't be long,' Guy promised. 'Stay there. You're not scared, are you, Kate?' he suggested with a wry twist of his wickedly beautiful mouth.

'Of course not.' She had all the same symptoms, though, Kate realised, staring back at him defiantly. Her heart was racing; her lungs were pumping.

'If you will just excuse me for a few moments,' he drawled, sketching a mock bow.

Hugging herself for comfort, Kate gazed around. The rows of plants seemed to stretch to infinity, but there were no dark corners so there was absolutely no need for her to be nervous, she told herself firmly as she hummed a tuneless little song. But as the minutes ticked by she thought more than once about tearing back up the stairs and out into the open air again.

'Thank you for waiting.'

She whirled around at the sound of Guy's voice, then uttered a short cry. 'Comtesse de Villeneuve!' Kate sped across to Guy's side where his mother stood leaning on her son's arm, but her attempt at a formal greeting was brushed aside as the Countess drew her into a warm embrace.

'Thank you so much for coming to the château, Kate, *chérie*. After the accident—' The Countess broke off and made a small gesture with one hand as if to signal her inability to discuss the tragedy. 'I only ever leave my room now to come down and see my plants,' she explained in a voice husky with emotion. 'Guy thought I might be on my way down. It's my usual time.'

'But you can't remain isolated like that,' Kate declared impulsively. 'You must come to the cottage and visit me.' She took the old lady's free hand in a firm grip and squeezed it encouragingly.

'I never leave the château,' the Countess explained apologetically, shaking her head. 'I don't feel safe—not since the accident.'

'You'll feel safe with me,' Kate promised fervently.

'We'll see,' the Countess said wistfully. 'Will you take me back now, Guy? Come with us, Kate. Guy will take you home when he has seen me to my room.'

On impulse, Kate lifted the Countess's hand to her lips. 'I've missed you,' she said shyly.

The Countess stroked her hand down Kate's hair as she studied her face with a still clear gaze. 'And I've missed you, my dear Kate. More than you know.'

'You look as if you've lost a penny and found a pound,' Megan exclaimed as they clashed pots together in the sink the next morning.

Kate touched her hands to her cheeks, remembering her visit with the Countess that had more than made up for her lapse of control with Guy. Fortunately, with his mother uppermost in both their minds, she had been spared his teasing on the drive home. Megan's face lit up at the news of Kate's encounter with the Countess. 'It might not be much,' she said wisely when Kate explained how short and unusual her visit had been, 'but it's the first small step towards recovery. Now we have to persuade her to visit us here at the cottage.'

'How's your migraine?' Kate enquired, although Megan looked as fit as a fiddle.

'Never mind that. Do I detect a feverish glow in those emerald eyes of yours?' Megan countered. 'And don't tell me that's a love-bite on your neck?' she said, furiously working the wire wool over the frying pan.

'I don't know what you imagine, but I can assure you that Guy has no romantic interest in me whatever. And, as for a love-bite—' Fat chance! Kate thought ruefully. 'I just rubbed myself too hard with the towel this morning after my shower.'

'If you say so—'

'I do say so.'

'Ah, well then.' Megan sighed. 'But did my little ruse work?' she demanded, keeping her eyes fixed resolutely on her task.

'Your little ruse?'

'That's right,' Megan said as she lifted her head to quiz Kate. 'You see, I thought that if I just left you with him...'

'You left me on purpose!' Kate exclaimed incredulously. 'How could you do that? How could you leave me alone with Guy?'

'I made such a mess of everything earlier—scattering those paint brushes—I just thought if I left the two of you alone together it would solve all your problems.'

Kate's facial expressions ran the gamut from surprise and then on to amusement as she realised what Megan was getting at. 'What? Buy him off with my body, you mean?'

'It's a thought...'

'Megan! If it was anyone but you...'

'Well, it isn't,' Megan said gruffly.

'I know,' Kate said, giving her a hug. 'You're as bad as ever.'

'I certainly hope so.'

'But, for your information…'

'Yes?' Megan prompted eagerly.

'Nothing happened,' Kate said flatly. And that was all she was prepared to admit, even if Megan was giving her one of her special narrowed eyes looks. And it was thanks to Guy's self-control rather than her own shaky willpower that she was able to make that proud assertion at all, she realised ruefully.

'Pity.'

'You're impossible, Megan O'Reilly.' Kate sighed with exasperation. 'Sleeping with Guy isn't the answer.'

'Not for you, maybe, but for every other woman on the planet.'

'He doesn't want me, I've told you that already,' Kate asserted, determined to shoot Megan's grand plan out of the sky once and for all. 'He's only playing games with me—just like he always has done. And, if following some extreme lapse of judgement I did sleep with him, how do you think he would react when he found out that I had pulled the wool over his eyes?'

'And you really think you can do that?'

'What?'

'Pull the wool over his eyes,' Megan said, clearly unconvinced.

'Well, I can try,' Kate said, feeling dejected too suddenly as she contemplated the enormity of the task she had set herself. It was one complication she could certainly do without.

'Have you not tried to talk him round?'

'There's no point,' Kate said. 'He's absolutely adamant.'

'Ah, well then.' Megan sighed with a frown. 'If direct confrontation won't work, we'll just have to let him get used to the idea slowly.'

It was perhaps as well Megan had no idea what they

were up against, Kate thought. Even without Guy's disapproval, it was one thing expecting Megan to see her way around the cottage with candles in the evening, but it was quite another to expect paying guests to do the same. 'Don't worry, I'll work something out,' she said, hoping to sound more confident than she felt.

'That's my girl.'

As she gave Megan a quick hug, Kate remembered how much was at stake for her friend. 'I'll show you,' she promised fiercely.

'Of course you will,' Megan murmured soothingly. 'Of course you will, my pet.'

The single imperative bleep of Kate's mobile phone drove them apart. 'I don't suppose you'd like to answer that?' Kate suggested wryly.

'Not a chance,' Megan retorted, matching her mood with a lopsided grin.

Kate hesitated a moment and then picked up the phone.

'Well?' Megan demanded after a lengthy period of thoughtful hums from Kate, mingled with some muted agreement. 'Who was it?'

'Madame Duplessis,' Kate revealed in a voice taut with surprise and pleasure. '*Madame le Comtesse* has asked whether she might pay us a short visit...'

'I told you,' Megan broke in excitedly. 'She's going to take the first step to recovery, thanks to you.'

'That's overstating my involvement,' Kate said. 'It was Guy who brought us together.'

'But it's up to us now to do all we can to help her,' Megan pointed out.

'I know,' Kate agreed.

'That poor woman hasn't been out of doors since the accident,' Megan went on, 'and that's more than six months ago now.'

'I'm as anxious about her as you are.'

'It's up to us to heal her spirit—bring her here and then...'

Megan's eyes were dancing with enthusiasm and Kate hated to bring her down to earth. 'Take her into our confidence?'

'Yes, why not?' Megan agreed passionately. 'Maybe she can talk Guy round for you.'

'No,' Kate said firmly. 'The last thing Guy's mother needs is to be drawn into a dispute between us.'

'She's made of stronger stuff than you think,' Megan said directly.

'I'm not prepared to risk upsetting her,' Kate said. 'And, whatever you say to try and make me feel better about all of this, just remember, I'm misleading her son.'

'Oh, pish!' Megan said dismissively. 'Guy will survive.'

'Maybe,' Kate murmured, unconvinced, wondering if her friendship with him would too. When she had inherited the property she had taken Guy's support for granted. Now she could see how rash she had been. But the last thing she had been expecting was for him to forbid her the right to develop the cottage as she wanted. Suddenly it seemed as if Aunt Alice's loving gesture might well backfire and be the one thing that drove Guy away from her. 'I can hardly pretend I don't know anything about the covenants,' Kate reasoned. 'But to be honest with you, Megan, I haven't even read through them properly yet...'

'What?' Megan exploded. 'Now, that really isn't like you, Kate. You must be either ill or in love.'

'I don't need to read them to know—Guy's issued more than enough warnings and I'm certain he's absolutely determined to enforce them,' Kate protested.

'Ach!' Megan said dismissively. 'Guy's used to issuing instructions, that's all—used to having them obeyed too, I dare say. But then he's been spared your company for ten years or so, Kate. He'll just have to get used to big-time confrontations all over again.'

Kate's laugh was dry and humourless. She knew it wasn't going to be that easy. Megan had no idea how strong-minded Guy could be when he had the bit between his teeth. But now the thought of Guy with anything between his teeth brought the blood rushing back to Kate's cheeks—something Megan picked up right away.

'Guy didn't—you know? Last night,' she began awkwardly.

'You didn't miss a thing after you were carted back here,' Kate said reassuringly.

'Carted back?' Megan exclaimed. 'Well, I suppose a taxi, however comfortable, can't compare with Guy's limousine.' Her eyes went dreamy for a moment. 'Not when that limousine is chauffered by a very nice man wearing uniform—and a cap, if you please.'

'I can see you enjoyed the night at least,' Kate said dryly.

'Don't try and tell me you didn't,' Megan countered shrewdly, and then her eyebrows lifted almost to her hairline when Kate's mobile rang again. 'Aren't you going to answer that?' she prompted, watching Kate hesitate.

'You've certainly perfected the art of the silent phone call,' Megan observed dryly when Kate finally broke the connection. 'And now have you taken the vow of silence?' she prompted hopefully, exhibiting more than her usual degree of amused frustration.

'I'm sorry,' Kate murmured distractedly, thinking about the call. Guy had been brief, noncommittal. On the face of it he had called just to make sure she had enjoyed the evening. Her thank-you note was already written and waiting to be posted. She had hoped to keep things formal. But in his voice she had detected a chord she hadn't heard before—hard to explain, but like a seedling in the grit. He was prepared to forgive her. He had taken for granted the fact that she would accede to his demands not to run a business at the cottage. After all, why should she? She had made plenty of money already. But Freedom Breaks was a lot more than just a commercial venture for her. It was a mission to bring life back to the cottage; to restore the sanctuary Aunt Alice had once created for her and to try and rebuild everything that had been lost six months earlier when Guy's father had come to take Aunt Alice to the château in his new car and had lost control… But that was all in the past. Guy's eye was on the future. And Kate knew his business plans didn't allow for sentimentality.

Suddenly she had to get away, to try and make sense of it all. 'Do you mind if I go for a walk?' she said distractedly. 'I won't be long.'

'Be as long as you like,' Megan said staunchly. 'There's plenty here I can be getting on with.'

Kate took herself off to the place where she had enjoyed her first impromptu picnic with Guy on her return to La Petite Maison. She needed to be alone and there was something therapeutic about the cottage and its lovely gardens, gardens that stretched down to the stream and, now that they were loved again, combined just the right degree of informality and design. She only had to walk through them to feel the benefit—to soak up the calm. The days were drawing out, becoming warmer, while the sounds and the scents around her were stronger, more evocative… Childhood seemed close, almost within reach.

Those long days in the sun, viewing Guy from a discreet distance as he talked with his friends… Listening to the pitch of his voice as it rose and fell against a background of bee drone and adoring female laughter. How she had hated them, Kate remembered—those beautiful girls, so grown up and so sophisticated and every one of them vying for Guy's attention, whilst she was still a child and a tomboy at that, with dirty knees and grass in her hair. But his voice had soothed her, lulled her, hypnotised her with its resonance and humour. And now since their talk at the château something much deeper than the tone of his voice was drawing her in. There was an intimacy between them that had not existed before. And with it came an understanding that only increased her longing to turn their lifelong friendship into something much more. But while he still saw her as a young tomboy that was never going to happen. She shook her head as she realised what a fool she had been.

It was one thing drawing up plans for the new business venture in an emotion free zone. It was equally insane to imagine that a relationship with Guy, Count de Villeneuve was ever going to be anything more than a light-hearted friendship... And if that friendship occasionally over-stepped the mark? Guy withdrew at the double and made it quite plain that it was only a momentary lapse, Kate reminded herself. But how could she remain unmoved, or do nothing, when she saw how the tragedy had shaken him to the very core—when she felt his pain as her own? It had been futile hoping to restore Aunt Alice's possessions; she could see that now. But the damage done by the accident to Guy and his mother was different; she could make at least some impression on that.

When Kate found her spot again she could almost imagine that no time had passed at all and that any moment Guy might arrive at the head of his troupe of friends. Kicking off her sandals, she sank on to a lush cushion of grass and wild herbs. Then, taking her time to select a succulent strand, she plucked it and, rolling on her back in the dappled sunlight, closed her eyes and began pensively to chew.

'Penny for them...'

'Guy!' Shading her eyes with her hands as she looked up at him, Kate saw that he looked even more handsome than he had in her mind's eye—and infinitely more desirable.

'What brings you here? No, don't get up. You look so comfortable there—so happy and contented. Are you happy, Kate?'

Guilt brought a frown to her face before she could do anything to stop it.

'No?' he queried softly, making her feel even worse with his concern.

'Guy, the covenants...' Kate began, determined to make an end of it there and then.

*'Pas maintenant,'* he said holding up his hands. 'I've had enough of business for one day.'

As he swiped a gloved hand across the back of his neck she saw the tension in his face and fell silent again. 'What are you doing here?' She could see he'd been riding. Riding hard, to judge by the state of his dust-streaked shirt. He tugged off his riding gloves and dropped them on the ground as she pulled herself up into a sitting position. She found herself facing legs planted either side of her, legs that were moulded in some close-fitting fabric that showed every contour and every curve of his hard muscles.

'I asked you first,' he reminded her.

Her throat felt dry. His voice was firm, demanding, his eyes narrowed in speculation as he waited for her answer. And when she stared into the sun and tried to summon up an explanation, he dropped to his knees beside her and took hold of her hands. 'Don't look so worried,' he insisted, a wry smile tugging at the corners of his mouth. 'It's a beautiful day. Be happy, Kate.'

She wanted to tell him then—tell him everything. But as he drew her close she could think of nothing except being in his arms. But his embrace was not the touch of a lover— it was something more, yet a lot less. It was something unique and precious, like the bittersweet kernel of happiness that blossomed inside her every time he was near, but it was controlled and chaste too, so that at the same time it answered all of her needs and none. But if this were all it could ever be, she would take it. 'I am happy,' she whispered, nestling into him, feeling his steady heartbeat against her face.

'Do you mind?' he said, letting her go at last to finger the buttons on his shirt.

'Mind?'

'If I take my shirt off.'

Kate longed to reach out to him and tackle each small tan horn button one by one…slowly. It didn't take much to imagine how it might feel to slide the black shirt off the wide sweep of his shoulders, to feel the warmth of his skin under her fingers, to become familiar with the texture and revel in the strength of him... And then she would release it from the waistband of his breeches...

'You're sure you don't mind?' he repeated.

'No, of course I don't mind,' she said, proud of herself for sounding so rational.

Guy gave a sigh of satisfaction as he tossed his shirt to one side. '*C'est bon,*' he said, contentedly stretching out beside her.

Did he have any idea—any idea at all? Kate wondered, trying not to make it obvious as she eyed his incredible physique. His legs she already knew about, having studied them in some detail—but his stomach, she saw now, was completely flat and like his broad chest banded with muscle. There was a shading of dark hair on his tanned chest whose narrowing strip drew the eye down to where it disappeared above the fastenings on the waistband of his breeches...and it was possible to see beyond that without even appearing to look. Kate gasped as he shifted position, but he was only picking out his own strand of grass to suck. As he slipped it between his firm lips, for one heady moment she considered launching herself at him—but she knew he would only make a joke of it, so she settled back with her head on the grass... Close enough to hear him breathing, but far enough away to keep a hold on what remained of her sanity.

'It was good to have you at the château last night,' he said lazily, almost as if it was too much effort to speak. 'Did you enjoy yourself?'

Had she enjoyed herself? How could she begin to tell him? Kate wondered, pausing before she spoke. 'It was a wonderful moment when your mother walked in.'

'As it was for her to see you,' Guy said softly. 'I can assure you of that.'

'And the meal was delicious, the wine too,' Kate said as every moment came flooding back in minute detail. 'And

the setting is superb, but then, of course, you know that.'
She stopped as he hummed a response that seemed to demand more from her. But what more could she say? When Megan had left for the cottage the air had been charged with something indefinable—something of her own conjuring, she knew that now. At the time she had thought it a tension they both felt—but now she knew she was wrong. Oh, he had kissed her—on the cheek when he took her home. But earlier, when she had tried to make it something more, he had taken her wrists in a careful grip and gently pushed her away. Of course, there was still the puzzle of that one kiss, the first kiss on her return... There had been nothing remotely chaste about that...

'Daydreaming, Kate?'

Now it was her turn to hum a noncommittal response that answered nothing.

'Last night,' Guy prompted patiently, leaning on one elbow to look down at her. 'Was it all right for you?'

Right question, wrong occasion, Kate thought ruefully, smothering a smile as she rolled away from him on to her stomach. 'I had a wonderful evening. So did Megan.'

'That's good,' Guy murmured, trailing a strand of grass across the back of her neck, 'because I'm thinking of asking you again.'

'Really?' Kate's heart was thumping as she turned to stare up at him.

'Yes, I thought I might show you the dungeons this time. What do you think?'

'The same dungeons Megan thinks you should be locked up in?' Kate said.

'The very same,' Guy admitted in a teasing drawl as he ran his strand of grass down her naked arm. His lips curved with satisfaction as he watched her quivering reaction. 'Still as sensitive as ever, Kate?' He sounded pleased.

It used to be called ticklish years back...and ticklish was a harmless definition, sensitive was not, Kate realised, as she indulged herself for a few private moments in the waves of arousal buffeting her senses. 'Tell me about your dungeons,' she said huskily, hoping to distract him. She relaxed her head down on to her folded arms and waited... After all, she told herself as she waited for him to embellish her erotic fantasies, she had never had the opportunity to visit them.

'They're dark and quiet and dry—' Guy began very softly as he turned his attention to the back of her neck again, brushing the soft red-gold hair aside as he began to pass the tip of the meadow grass across the warm translucent skin with slow rhythmical strokes '—and warm and extremely private.'

'And what happens in them these days?' She could barely stop herself moving on the warm earth so immense was the sensual overload.

'That all depends on who's in there at the time,' Guy murmured.

Kate held her breath. She could feel his warm breath on her ear, ruffling her hair, caressing her skin—surely this was the moment...

'Shall we paddle?'

'Paddle?' Brutally jolted out of her reverie, Kate could only roll over and stare up at him in surprise.

But even that was a mistake, because now Guy was above her and she was under his shadow with nowhere else to look but straight into his eyes. He had positioned himself as if he might kiss her—he only had to lower himself down an inch or two and...

'I think the cold water would refresh us both,' he said, pulling away to sit on his haunches. Then, springing to his feet, he toed off his riding boots and yelled, 'Come on, Kate. Last one into the water's a sissy!'

Kate's limbs felt as if they had rubber where bones used to be and there was so much heat between her thighs she was almost more eager than he was to reach the safety of the water... At least there he wouldn't know that her thong was so wet she was concerned the proof of the effect he had on her might soak right through the thin muslin skirt. In her rush to get there she tore heedlessly down the bank after him, lost her footing and would have gone flying past him to land on the heaps of stones that lined the water's edge if Guy hadn't reached out to catch her in his arms.

'You never could bear to lose a dare,' he said, his face close above hers as he held her suspended above the water.'

'Let me go!' Kate insisted, struggling fiercely. And he did. Dropping her at his feet so that for a moment she was completely submerged. 'Beast!' she railed, springing up to launch herself at him. She was lucky. She caught him off-balance and before either of them could do anything about it they were both flat on their backs under the water. Guy recovered first, pulling her to her feet in front of him with a harsh, very masculine laugh.

'In the olden days I could have had you locked up in my dungeons for that,' he observed, his even white teeth a visible line of masculine pride in his strong tanned face as he held her at arm's length in front of him. 'Or flogged—'

'You wouldn't dare!' Kate flared back at him.

For a moment they just stood there passionate and wild, all identity stripped away as they confronted each other in the middle of the stream. The air was electric between them. Kate's clothes were soaking and proved that she wore nothing underneath except for her tiny thong and Guy, with his thick black hair flicked around the harsh planes of his wet cheeks, bare-chested with his breeches like a second skin, looked like some wild gypsy baron, rather than the educated French aristocrat he was. Then with a shriek of defiance, Kate launched a kick that doused him with water again. Seeing the look on his face she shrieked again, this time with excitement as the chase began.

He let her get away at first—he always had. But then he ran her down at the entrance to the glade—Kate's glade— the silent, leafy place where she'd used to hide as a child. Once she was inside the circle of trees it was possible to believe she had found some mystical Neverland where no one ever came—where even the birdsong was muted and the sunlight was only allowed to intrude if it came dressed in shimmering shafts of light... Slides for fairies, Kate used to think once, as she gazed up their slopes. Now she kicked her legs through them in furious defiance as Guy carried her in his arms across the clearing.

'Now what do I do with you?' he demanded, setting her down at his feet on a rolling green carpet of moss.

'Let me go,' she muttered mutinously.

'I've got a better idea,' he said, dropping to his knees beside her.

'Which is?' Kate demanded as she threw a cascade of tousled golden hair back from her face.

'This,' he said simply, drawing her into his arms.

# CHAPTER SEVEN

KATE was still riding the wave of passion and excitement from the chase and it only took the smallest shift for that energy to change direction. The touch of Guy's hard chest against the scant protection of her wet blouse was enough. And this time she was on an unstoppable rollercoaster ride that swept every rule aside. With a sharp cry of intent she lashed her arms around his neck in an attempt to put an end to the torment once and for all. Why not kiss him and make him kiss her back? But he only caught hold of her wrists and forced her back—back and away from him until she lay panting and spent on the mossy bed by his side.

'Did you really think I would allow you to take advantage of me?' he demanded, delivering the rebuke in a fierce, teasing voice.

He was so close she could see the tiny aquamarine flecks in his dazzling grey eyes—so close they seemed to share the same breath, the same air. 'Take advantage of you!' Kate gasped, knowing she was pinned so securely he could do anything with her he liked. 'Let me go—let me go!' she exclaimed, fighting to stop her gaze lingering on his mouth. But he had captured her wrists in one hand, whilst his other posed a delicious threat as it hovered over her, reducing her to writhing on the ground, to his obvious entertainment.

'How can I let you go?' he said, as if there might have been the slightest chance he would. 'Wild-cats must be tamed.'

With a throaty explosion of frustration made sound, she lay still.

Guy's eyes mirrored his thought processes, Kate realised as she watched a kaleidoscopic display of infinitesimal

116

changes taking place in their silvery depths. So when his gaze darkened she knew the cause. The girl was left behind at last as he saw her as the woman she had become. It was an awakening for him, a revelation that brought a softening to his features Kate had never seen before. Releasing her, he took her face in his hands. The stillness surrounding them seemed absolute, as if all nature held its breath. And then, as if to endorse his discovery, Guy lowered his head and pressed the firm cushion of his lips against her slightly open mouth. It was at once the most sensitive and the most sensuous experience Kate had ever known.

'Is that what you wanted, Kate?' he murmured, lifting his head away without making the slightest attempt to deepen the kiss. 'Or perhaps this…*ceci*?' As his hands moved to feather caresses on either side of her neck she drew in a sharp breath, but now he was trailing his fingertips over every curve and indentation of her naked shoulders. Through it all he watched intently as she tried vainly to curb the betraying movement of her hips. 'Perhaps not,' he murmured as his gaze shifted to her erect nipples competing for his attention beneath the clinging blouse.

Through the miasma of arousal Kate was aware she had him in her sway. The game was far from over yet. Willing ice through her veins, she managed somehow to sit up. Her gaze was an outright challenge. She watched in triumph as Guy failed to keep his gaze level. It strayed to the ruby upthrust of nipples taunting him from beneath the revealing, wet fabric. But, just as she was complimenting herself on reclaiming the advantage, he threw back his head and gave a laugh that rippled through her body like a seismic tremor.

'You'd like that, wouldn't you, sweet Kate?' he murmured, maintaining a tantalising distance between them.

'What do you mean?' In spite of Kate's attempt to launch herself back into the fray, her voice sounded about as steady as a feather on a breath of wind. 'I don't understand what you're trying to say.'

'Then allow me to enlighten you,' Guy murmured as he

wound a damp tendril of Titian hair round his finger like a tether. 'I think you'd like to see me lose control…bend to your will…serve you like some plundering stallion.'

'No!' His suggestion was outrageous—and so was its effect on her senses. Before she had a chance to recover he captured her chin in his hand.

'I disagree,' he said in low, harsh tone. 'I think that's exactly what you'd like me to do. *Mais*—' He shook his head in mock-regret. 'It isn't going to be like that, Kate.' Then, keeping her trapped in his gaze, he kissed her—just a frustrating brush of his lips accompanied by a sharp warning sound of denial when she tried to urge him on. 'My way,' he insisted softly when she sighed her complaint. 'Or no way.' But his way was gathering strength all the time, and a soft moan escaped Kate's throat when a deep throb of pleasure accompanied his tongue's possession of her mouth. Refusing her the firmer touch of his hands, Guy continued to ravish her mouth with a skill that left her weak, plunging and withdrawing in a provocative game of advance and retreat that effortlessly crowned her own in-expert tactics. 'Better, Kate?' he murmured sardonically as he lifted his head. 'Or still not quite enough for you?'

'I think you know the answer to that,' she said huskily against the corner of his mouth, moulding herself to him when he kissed her again.

As if he could not bear to be removed from her lips for a moment, Guy helped her to take off the sodden blouse while they kissed. As soon as she was free his hands moved to claim her breasts. Then, swinging down flat on the ground, he brought her on top of him, still holding her away so that her tortured nipples were only inches from his face. 'Now feed me,' he ordered softly, his sweeping sable brows lifting in sardonic challenge. Gently and slowly he brought her down until Kate could feed one engorged tip between his lips. He took the other side himself, rolling the sensitive bud over and over between his tongue and his lips until she thought she'd go mad for him. But he showed her no mercy at all and only brought her legs round to straddle him so that she felt the unmistakable heat and thrust of his erection pulsing against her. She wanted him. Oh, how she wanted him.

But the moment he moved her skirt, she said, 'No!' and flinched back.

'*Non?*' Guy queried softly, hearing the panic in her voice.

'No, I can't... I just can't.' Shaking her head, Kate pulled away from him. Going to sit on her own a few feet away she drew her knees up and, wrapping her arms around them, she buried her face in her lap.

'What's wrong?' Guy said, putting a protective arm around her shoulders. 'Tell me, Kate. What's the matter?'

'I just can't, that's all,' she said, burying her face deeper.

'Look at me,' he insisted gently. '*Non*, Kate,' he said sharply when she turned away. 'Look at me, Kate. Don't turn away. Something's upset you and you must tell me what it is.'

Still with her head buried on her knees, she turned her face just enough to mutter, 'My damaged leg—it's ugly.'

Guy stayed very still for a few moments then gently brought her round to face him. 'Kate, Kate, courageous Kate,' he murmured tenderly, 'let me assure you that there is not one part of you I could possibly find ugly.'

'There is,' she argued, her eyes clouding with certainty.

'Show me,' he said simply.

'I can't.'

Laying her down flat on the ground beside him, Guy peeled back the soaking skirt to expose a scar that snaked down her left leg almost to the knee.

'I had to have a plate put in after the accident,' Kate explained tonelessly. 'Now tell me it isn't ugly.'

'I think you're beautiful,' Guy said. 'And that means every part of you. This doesn't make any difference to me at all. I still think you're beautiful.' And, dipping his head, he planted kisses all the way down the fine silvery line.

'Come to me,' he said, drawing her into his arms. 'Just lie quietly with me here and forget everything that happened—put everything out of your mind except for the fact that you've come back to me—back to France where I'll never let anything hurt you again.'

Guy had seen the wound on her leg now, Kate thought as tears began to run unseen by him down her cheeks, but he couldn't see the wound that his trust had just carved in her heart.

'And where have you been?' Megan demanded fondly when Kate returned to the cottage shortly before dusk. 'A walk, you said. Not a ruddy marathon. And look at you! Your skirt's a mess. Are you all right?'

Glancing down ruefully at her clothes, Kate hardly knew where to begin. 'I'm fine,' she said as a catch-all. 'Stop worrying about me, Megan. I'm a big girl now.'

'Oh, really.' Megan sighed, clearly unconvinced.

'I met Guy…'

'Now you do surprise me,' Megan murmured.

'I fell in the stream…'

'And he fished you out.'

'Pretty much.'

'Nothing hurt?'

'Only my pride.'

'Well, that's good, because I've got some news for you.'

From the way Megan was assessing her reaction with sneaky looks in the mirror whilst pretending to be fully occupied checking out the sets of paintbrushes she was arranging on the worktop, Kate thought the news might not be good. 'Go on.'

'Three of our guests phoned to ask if they could arrive a little early—so I telephoned the others and asked…'

'Oh, Megan, you didn't…'

'As we are going to be welcoming half the neighbourhood to our opening bash I thought it would be a grand occasion they shouldn't miss.'

'You did?' Kate said, throwing Megan a look of fond exasperation.

'I did,' Megan admitted, shooting Kate a look through her lashes to see if she was forgiven. 'Well, it's in at the deep end, pet. And that's by far the best way, if you ask me. I can't bear to see you getting so worked up over this business. After all these years you should know better than anyone that there's not a person alive who could put one over on young Guy. Why don't you just come clean and tell him you intend to run a guest house…?'

'No, Megan,' Kate said firmly. 'I can assure you…'

'Assure me all you like,' Megan broke in flatly. 'But he's as stubborn as you are and he's got a lot on his plate at the moment, what with restoring the château, recovering the business and worrying about his mother. As far as I'm concerned, the sooner everything's out in the open, the better.'

'Like you said, he's got enough on his plate,' Kate said. 'And where should I confront him, do you think—in front of our first guests?'

'And half the village,' Megan reminded Kate gaily, refusing to be discouraged.

'I'm sorry,' Kate said, putting an arm around Megan's shoulders to give her a hug. 'I know you're right. I just can't seem to find the right moment… And you can stop looking at me like that,' she said, trying not to smile when Megan's eyebrows shot up. OK, Kate thought wryly, so she would add crisis management to her list of accomplishments. Mentally rolling up her sleeves, she ran quickly through a checklist. 'Any news of the electricity?'

'Not a word,' Megan said.

'Right, leave that to me. Are you ready to roll?'

'As I'll ever be,' Megan confirmed.

'And I can easily bring forward my order for fresh vegetables from the château,' Kate murmured thoughtfully, 'so that's not a problem.' And Guy had said he was going away for a few days, so what on earth was she worrying about?

By the time he got back everything would be working

like clockwork. 'I'm glad you said our guests could come earlier, Megan. Suddenly I can't wait to get this new business of ours up and running.'

Just a few days later the first guests' arrival at La Petite Maison took Kate completely by surprise. Megan was in the back garden, setting up some easels under a canopy where she planned to allow the children from the village to test their artistic skills at the party, while Kate was busy in the kitchen preparing food with her long hair piled up and secured by a piece of vivid emerald-green chiffon. She had covered her simple working clothes with one of her capacious white aprons whose patch pockets contained all sorts of essential items, from a ball of string to a corkscrew. The windows and the doors had been left open so that she and Megan could exchange news on their individual progress at the shout, and fragrant cooking aromas had been escaping for hours so that the cottage was enveloped in a cocoon of mouthwateringly good smells.

Kate was so wrapped up in piping a decoration on top of one of her cakes that she missed the first timid knock, but a second, louder tap called her attention to the door. Putting down the piping bag, she called out, 'Come straight in,' then hurried to the door, wiping her hands on the front of her apron as she went. *'Madame la Comtesse!'* she exclaimed, amazed to see Guy's mother on the threshold, accompanied by Madame Duplessis.

'Ah, I knew it would be inconvenient,' the Dowager Countess exclaimed, taking a step backward as she put a lace-gloved hand to her mouth.

'Not at all,' Kate insisted, standing back encouragingly.

'Well—if you're sure,' the elderly lady said hesitantly, peering curiously past Kate into the room. 'Only there is so much talk…I couldn't resist coming to see what all the fuss is about. Not that I listen to gossip,' she said quickly. 'It's just that everyone is so excited about the party…' She trailed off with a wistful, 'And I shan't be there…'

'But why shouldn't you come?' Kate said, flashing a look at Madame Duplessis, whom she hoped would back her up. Before Madame Duplessis had a chance to speak, Megan bustled back inside.

'Why not indeed?' Megan declared.

'Megan? What are you doing here?' the Countess said, reaching out as if she couldn't quite believe her eyes.

'I'm here to inject a little chaos into Kate's well-ordered home,' Megan informed her as she took hold of the Countess's hands in her warm grip and raised them to her lips. 'You look pale,' she said with her customary frankness.

'Ah, well.' The Countess sighed dismissively. 'They're saying I should come to this party. What do you think about it, Megan?'

'What harm could it do?' Megan said frankly.

The Countess looked from one to the other as if seeking reassurance from them all. 'Oh, no,' she protested, fluttering her hands. 'I'm far too old for that sort of thing.'

'Nonsense,' Kate insisted as she removed her apron. 'And, as a matter of fact, I could do with some help.' Ignoring Madame Duplessis's shocked look, Kate continued to give voice to her plan as she escorted the Countess across the room to the most comfortable chair. 'You see, *madame*, there will be many more people than I had imagined at first...'

'The place will be overrun,' Megan cut in enthusiastically. 'We're desperate for help...'

'I could help,' Madame Duplessis offered, looking quickly at the Countess for confirmation.

'We both could,' the Countess of Villeneuve declared firmly as she settled herself down on to the plump cushions. 'There was a time when I held parties twice a year for everyone in the village... You remember, Megan? I know you came once or twice with dear Alice...' She stopped and had to recover her composure. 'But Kate,' she said at last, injecting some vigour into the sadness, 'you must tell us what to do.'

'That was a good move of yours,' Megan declared later over supper when they were alone. 'You accomplished more than all the doctors could with that one suggestion to the Countess.'

Kate brushed off the praise with a small gesture as she heaped Megan's plate with a second slice of still warm cherry *clafoutis*. 'Cream?' Adding a little pouring cream, she passed the sugar-dusted, crisp and creamy batter pudding across the table to Megan. Then, easing back in her chair, she smothered a yawn. 'I was just so thrilled to see the sparkle back in her eyes again. I only hope she knows what she's taking on. Do you think we're ready, Megan?'

Glancing round the kitchen, Megan smiled. 'I know we are.'

Every available surface was stacked high with Kate's delectable cakes and pastries, and plenty more had been taken back to the château to be stored overnight in the massive refrigerators.

'No wonder you're tired,' Megan said sympathetically. 'You've made enough to feed half of France, never mind half the village.'

'I just didn't want them to be disappointed.'

Megan made a scoffing noise. 'No chance of that.'

'And I wanted to make a good impression on our first guests,' Kate added, making a final mental check on the bedrooms. 'Fresh flowers—'

'What's that?'

'Fresh flowers for the bedrooms and around the cottage,' Kate said, looking worried suddenly. 'I completely forgot— and I'd like some for the table outside.' She planned to present much of the food on one long table in the garden. The Countess had offered several trestle tables that could be placed together to fit her needs, but the flowers—

'Marie Therese said...' Megan began.

'Marie Therese?' Kate said, her mouth curving in a wry smile. 'My, we are on good terms.'

'The Countess expressly asked me to call her by her first name, just like your aunt used to do,' Megan revealed, her plump cheeks flushing pink as she revealed this development.

'Well, go on then,' Kate encouraged. 'What did Marie Therese say to you?' she enquired, her happy emerald eyes glowing like jewels.

'She said we could have the pick of her nurseries and the garden,' Megan said with a contented flourish as she forked up the last scrap of her dessert.

'But that's wonderful!' Kate said, mentally erasing another worry. 'So,' she said thoughtfully. 'Our first house-guests arrive just before noon…and everyone else will be here shortly after that.'

'That's right,' Megan said, watching Kate's face, knowing they had set themselves an almost impossibly tight schedule.

But in spite of all the problems, not least of which was the possibility that Guy could turn up unannounced, Kate felt a rush of incredible excitement rather than apprehension. 'Then I think we'd better get to bed,' she said with a last glance around. 'It's going to be a hectic day tomorrow.'

'You can say that again,' Megan muttered as she started blowing out candles. 'And I only hope you're right about our guests finding the lack of electricity a novelty.'

'As long as they have plenty of hot water they'll be fine,' Kate said confidently, 'and the old range is firing on all cylinders since Giles came to service it.'

'I hope you're right,' Megan repeated as she handed Kate a candle to light her way upstairs. 'And I hope they're careful. The last thing we need is another fire.'

'Don't tell me you're having second thoughts, Megan,' Kate said wryly. 'I told you Guy promised to sort out the electrical supply if I hadn't managed to influence the local authorities by the time he returned home from his business trip.'

'He told you this during that fishing trip of his, I suppose. The same fishing trip where you disappeared off on that walk and returned home looking like a love-struck mermaid? Yes, I remember,' Megan said dryly. 'And will you be telling him why you need the electricity so badly?'

'I'll think of something,' Kate said distractedly, knowing that Megan had just guaranteed her a sleepless night.

Three anxious-looking elderly spinsters from the dramatically desolate Pennine region in the North of England, one ashen-faced retired rocker from Bermondsey and an exotically dressed middle-aged man with more facial hair than Father Christmas constituted something less, and yet, at the same time, rather more than the high-flying executives Kate had envisaged for her first guests after advertising La Petite Maison in the business section of one of the broadsheets. Fortunately, Megan took it all in her stride.

'It couldn't have worked out better,' she declared, leaning over Kate's shoulder to peer out of the window at them. 'They're an interesting group of people and they won't be so edgy. And, my word, those men certainly add some colour!' She squinted professionally along her paintbrush as they both stared at the gold brocade caftan of one and the fit-where-they-touch, shiny vinyl pants of the other.

'It couldn't have worked out better?' Kate echoed. 'And how do you make that out?' she said as she loaded some tumblers on to a tray. 'They'll hardly blend in. How am I going to explain them to the Countess?'

'Say they're house guests,' Megan suggested promptly. 'Well, it's true,' she added as she turned to greet the three ladies, who were just coming down the stairs. Far from being alarmed by the lack of electricity, they had declared themselves enchanted by the rustic charm of the cottage.

'Now, wait a minute,' Megan said, stalling midway across the room. 'Who's that I see coming up the path?'

'Oh, no.' Kate's poise slipped as she followed Megan's gaze. 'I don't believe it.' As her heart took off at the sight of Guy striding towards the front door, she became vaguely but very thankfully aware that Megan had the good sense to usher their three female visitors out of the back door.

A distinctive rap sounded on the door, then Guy walked into the kitchen. 'Kate—'

'Guy!' she exclaimed rather too energetically. 'What a surprise!'

'Is it?' he said curiously. 'I have got the right day, haven't I?' And, when she looked at him blankly, he added a reminder, 'Your house-warming party?'

So, he had made it after all... The fact that her heart was roaring in her ears had nothing whatever to do with the fact that her first house guests were currently walking right by the window, Kate realised, as she shifted position so that he was forced to look in the opposite direction. 'Oh, yes...yes, of course,' she said, trying not to accept that her throat had dried just at the sight of him in his casual linen suit and crisp white shirt. 'I'm sorry,' she said, clapping her hands together in pretended recovery. 'Of course I'm expecting you. I'm not quite ready yet, that's all.'

'Good,' he said, oblivious to the sexual waves with which he was flooding out her kitchen. 'Well, I'm glad I got here before everyone else because I've got a surprise for you. *Bien*, aren't you going to ask me what it is?'

Kate tried to answer, but the words wouldn't come.

'Don't look so worried,' he said with a smile that would have melted a heart of stone, but only succeeded in making Kate stand rigid in an attempt to hide her feelings. 'It's just the man to connect the electricity for you,' he said, sounding pleased with himself, patently unaware of the riot he was causing to her senses. 'I brought him with me so there could be no mistake and no more delays. I left him up at that small electrical station on the hill, where he's sorting out the supply for you right now.'

'Oh, wonderful…' Kate said, wondering insanely if he could hear her heart jangling in her chest.

Almost as if drawn by invisible hands, Guy moved slowly past her to stare out of the window.

'Who are those people?' he said mildly. 'I don't think I recognise them.'

'Which people?' Kate said, hearing her voice come out in a squeak.

'Are they actors come to entertain at the party?'

She realised she was wringing her hands in alarm—and Guy could read body language with the best of them, Kate realised, shoving them behind her back fast.

'Or are they perhaps—' it was like being held by her ankles over hot coals, Kate thought as she waited for him to finish '—paying guests, Kate?' The edge in his voice wasn't half as effective as the prolonged silence that came after the accusation.

'Well?' he demanded quietly. 'Don't you think you owe me an explanation?'

There was something approaching menace in his voice and it rattled Kate's faltering hold on composure. 'You said you wouldn't mind my opening an office,' she reasoned, gulping hard.

'An office, no,' Guy agreed in the same measured tone.

'So? Is this so different?'

'Is what so different?'

'My guest house.'

'Your what?' he spat out.

'You heard me,' Kate insisted, drawing herself up. She would not be intimidated—she would not. His arms shot out like two steel girders, keeping her imprisoned with her back against the counter.

'The covenants on La Petite Maison do not permit it,' he growled very close to her face.

The force of his stare would have been enough to make

most people fall to their knees and beg for mercy, but Kate had seen that look before. Tossing up her head, she confronted the molten steel gaze unblinking. 'Well, I didn't know anything about your wretched covenants when I started to plan all this and now it's too late to do anything about it.'

'You obviously haven't read through those documents I gave you... Well, have you, Kate?' he demanded fiercely. 'And you might have done better to make some enquiries before you started planning your new venture,' he said curtly. 'But you know what really annoys me?' he added, staring straight into her eyes, and as Kate shook her head dumbly, he went on, 'The fact that you couldn't be honest with me—that you couldn't trust me enough to tell me about these plans of yours.'

'Perhaps if you hadn't kept on about those wretched covenants—'

'This has nothing to do with covenants, Kate, and you know it,' Guy snapped back at her. 'This is about trust.'

He kept her trapped in front of him, forcing her to draw her head back from the heat in his gaze.

'Trust between two people,' he continued, 'requires that they are straight with each other. Don't shake your head at me like that, as if you haven't the slightest idea what I'm talking about...'

'I don't,' Kate ground out miserably, wondering how long it would be before his anger was tainted by contempt.

'Well, I'll explain,' Guy promised tersely. 'You trusted me with your body, but when it comes to your life, you shut me out. What sort of woman does that, Kate?'

His accusation was stunning in its ferocity and Kate's head felt as if it was being held inside a steel vice and where there had been fire in her veins now there was only ice. 'I don't understand...'

'*Non*, Kate,' Guy corrected her bitterly. '*I'm* the one who doesn't understand. Did you really think I was such a monster?'

'So, how do you feel about my plans?' she challenged.

'Furious now,' he admitted frankly. 'I'm not going to let it happen.'

'But it *is* happening,' Kate pointed out, wishing she could sound a bit more sure of that.

With a gust of impatience, Guy wheeled away from her. He took a couple of strides across the room, where he drew to a halt with his back to her and swiped one tense hand across the back of his neck. 'This isn't a game, Kate. You aren't a little girl now. You can't just arrive in Villeneuve after all these years and turn everything here upside down.'

The passion in his voice frightened her. 'And is that what I'm doing?' Kate demanded softly.

'You know you are,' Guy murmured without turning around.

She longed to go to him, to say how sorry she was and ask if they could begin all over again. But the deep-rooted reserve she had always felt, being lower on the social scale than the Count de Villeneuve, held her back. He turned very slowly and stood in silence looking at her, his face a mask that told her nothing.

'There's no time to discuss this now,' he said decisively. 'You have guests waiting outside and more are due to arrive at any moment.'

'That's right,' Kate agreed, holding her breath to see what he would say next.

'Just remember, Kate. These estates and the people who depend upon them don't exist for my pleasure. I serve the Villeneuve estate and everyone connected with it. It's up to me to ensure that the environment in which we all live—'

'Is sterile?' she cut in.

He looked hurt by the remark. 'I cannot allow you to run a guest house here,' he said flatly.

'And I cannot allow you to tell me what to do,' Kate retorted, returning to the fray.

'Perhaps if you had read those damned documents you would understand—'

'Understand what?' she said, shaking her head with frustration.

'There's no time,' Guy said tensely. 'The future of the Villeneuve estate may mean nothing to you, Kate. But it's my life.'

'And a pretty boring one with no characters in it,' she pointed out stubbornly.

'There are more than enough characters in the village without you importing any more,' Guy informed her as he flared a glance out of the window. 'Those covenants stand, and if you can't, or won't, live by them—'

'What? Get out?' Kate suggested angrily. She watched his jaw clench as he bit back the words that were clearly clamouring in his head. Guy wasn't used to being countermanded. She could see his iron will flexing from every angle in the mirrors over the counter; his eyes were narrowed, his mouth a firm line, jaw tight and the magnificent spread of his shoulders were raised in a tense pose as he braced his hands against the side to watch Megan showing the others round the garden.

'No, not that,' he murmured to himself. 'That would be far too easy for you.'

What did he really see? Kate wondered as she followed his gaze. Could Guy see La Petite Maison already working its magic on those six people outside, as she could? Did he hear their laughter, see the animation in their faces, the glow of anticipation in their eyes? How would he feel when he knew his own mother…?

He pulled away from the counter at last and stared down at her.

'I can't stop this now,' Kate said tensely. 'I know you're angry with me, but—'

'I'm more disappointed than angry,' he said honestly, 'that you didn't see fit to share your plans with me.'

His anger wouldn't have hurt so much, Kate realised.

But what she had told him was true—she couldn't turn back now. There were too many hopes invested in La Petite Maison. She only had to think of what Megan had given up. 'If you force me to, I'll fight you every inch of the way.'

'Of that I have no doubt,' he murmured.

For a few moments nothing seemed to exist beyond the drama being played out between them. Kate felt exhausted by it before she started.

'You'd better get ready,' Guy said, reading her mood. 'Everyone will be here soon.'

'So you won't…?' Her voice tailed away as she looked up at him.

'I won't spoil your party,' he confirmed. A shadow briefly crossed his face, as if he was fighting an internal battle—almost as if part of him wanted her to succeed. 'I can see how much effort you've put into this,' he said as his glance took in the beautifully presented dishes of food covering every available surface. 'We'll talk about La Petite Maison some other time—soon,' he added, as if to prove to her that the problem wouldn't just go away.

'Thank you,' Kate said simply. 'Will you stay?'

'Stay?'

'Yes, for the party. Why not?'

'If I do,' Guy reasoned aloud, 'it will appear to everyone that I am endorsing your decision to open a guest house on the estate.'

'And if you don't,' Kate argued, 'the villagers will wonder why you do not wish to share this happy occasion with them.'

'Oh, Kate…you've no idea, have you?' He pressed his firm lips together as he looked at her and she saw the familiar mix of indulgence and frustration in his keen grey eyes. 'I'd be no use to you here, anyway,' he said, as if trying to convince himself.

'I disagree.'

'Of course you do,' he said dryly. 'Force of habit.'

A small answering smile touched her lips as she saw the suspicion of a smile starting to tug at the corners of his mouth.

'*Allez,*' he said softly, in a voice that made her ready to walk over hot coals for him if he asked. 'Go and get ready for your guests.'

'You'll still be here when I get back?'

His jaw worked and he said nothing, only his sweeping brows rose minutely, as if he was pleased she had asked the question.

As she walked away from him, Kate felt the intensity of his stare following her every move—scorching a trail between her shoulder blades. She had no idea whether he would still be there when she had freshened up, but there was no doubt in her mind at all that this business between them was going to run and run.

# CHAPTER EIGHT

THERE was no time to dwell on Guy's disapproval. The moment Kate returned downstairs she was thrown into the thick of things. While she had been getting ready the whole village seemed to have descended on the cottage. She felt a stab of disappointment when she saw the kitchen was deserted, with no sign of Guy. But hearing a steady rumble of conversation outside, punctuated by laughter and shouts of recognition, she knew she had to get over it. She had shed her working outfit in favour of a simple linen dress in a soft shade of lavender and, having brushed out her long hair in frantic haste, she'd chosen the fastest option, leaving it loose to billow around her shoulders in a bright golden haze.

The strong afternoon sunlight was already mellowing into a rich apricot glow as she hurried to remove some warm apple brioche out of the warming oven. After dusting the sweet bread with icing sugar, she slipped it on to a large oval dish and placed it on to a tray, ready to go outside. Hovering for a moment by the window, Kate couldn't help smiling to see Monsieur Dupont, missing only his badge of office—his crisp white jacket—holding court with the new arrivals clustered around him... Then she spotted Giles's wife, Elise, chatting with Megan, and Madame Duplessis actually flushing with pleasure as she held the attention of the brawny young village blacksmith. And someone had thought to bring an accordion, and was playing so well that a few people had already started dancing on the stone-flagged patio.

The party was a success, she realised happily. And best of all, she decided as her gaze rested upon a tiny, but elegant figure, Guy's mother was moving around the garden, offering titbits to the villagers and basking in their obvious delight at seeing her again—the men whipping off their hats and the women's eyes full of pleasure to see this evidence of her recovery. Food was a great icebreaker, Kate mused, as she lifted out a large plastic container of her own cardamom ice-cream from one of the cooler bags Madame Duplessis had thought to bring over from the château. Putting the ice cream and a scoop next to the brioche, she opened the door, picked up the tray and hurried outside.

'Félicitations!'

'Guy! I thought you'd gone.' Kate tensed as she gazed up, then relaxed into bemused speculation as she weighed up his outfit. His strong tanned arms shaded with dark hair and ornamented by nothing more than a slim gold watch on a black leather strap were now adorned with a tea towel! 'What on earth are you doing with that?' she said, noticing a second one he'd tied around his waist to cover his linen trousers. After all that had happened, his narrow-eyed look of wry indulgence was all the more surprising.

'Someone had to take charge of the barbecue,' he said dryly. 'You surely didn't think I'd leave it to Megan...?'

'Why not? She's perfectly capable.' Kate's heart jumped when she saw a humorous twist tug at his lips.

'When she's not distracted, I'd agree with you,' Guy agreed evenly. 'But right now...'

He shrugged and as Kate followed his gaze she saw Guy's chauffeur busily plying Megan with morsels of cake from his plate.

'I've heard of angel cake, but never Cupid's,' Guy murmured as he removed the tray from her hands.

When the villagers saw their Count bearing down on them with yet more delectable food a space was quickly cleared on the table for him and a queue formed for the pudding. Elise hurried over to take care of the serving, and then Guy found that his place at the barbecue had also been supplanted, this time by Monsieur Dupont. Just behind the barbecue an old feed trough had been packed with ice and filled with bottles of wine. Tossing his temporary apron aside, Guy filled up two glasses and returned to Kate's side.

'*Buves ceci,*' he said, pressing the glass into her hand. 'You look like you could use it.'

As compliments went, she'd heard better, but at least he was true to his word. Not only was he behaving as if no dispute existed between them, but he'd stayed on to help and had entered into the spirit of the party... So calm down, Kate told herself. 'Thank you, it's delicious,' she murmured, keeping her eyes safely fixed on the pale golden liquid.

'What can you smell?' Guy demanded, jolting her attention back to his face when she had been so resolved not to succumb.

'It's your wine?'

'*Naturellement,*' he said expansively. 'Now, concentrate and tell me what aromas you can detect.'

'Concentrate?' Was he joking?

'I'll show you,' Guy said, putting his own glass down. Coming to stand behind her, he put his hand over hers and held the glass up so that it was well out in front of her. '*Belle robe!*' he exclaimed softly.

'You like my dress?' Kate queried uncertainly, intensely conscious of the pulse that seemed to be throbbing through her hand, a pulse she was sure he must feel too.

'In this context,' he murmured, 'I am remarking on the beautiful colour of the wine.'

'I see,' Kate said, attempting studious attention when she was sure the quality of her voice was enough to give her away.

'Now we swirl and sniff.'

'We do?'

After a quick rotation of the glass, Guy reached under her long hair with his other hand to find the sensitive area at the back of her neck, his thumb controlling, his fingers splaying to nurse her scalp. 'Breathe in through your nose,' he commanded softly, encouraging her forward, 'and then tell me what you have discovered.'

Nothing she could safely tell him about, Kate thought ruefully as she obeyed him.

'Well, Kate?' he demanded, clearly expecting some erudite comment.

'Er... Honey, melon...sunshine?' she added in desperation.

'Très bien,' he drawled.

His praise thrilled through her and, considering the exceptional circumstances, Kate couldn't help feeling rather pleased with herself.

'Now sip,' he instructed as he brought the glass to her lips.

'Can I swallow?'

His look was X-rated. 'I'll leave that up to you,' he murmured dryly.

'Mmm, delicious,' she said, flashing him a wide-eyed look.

'Here, let me take that,' Guy said, removing the glass from her hand, his face a mask of beautifully controlled amusement. 'Shall we dance?'

'Dance?'

'Yes, you know,' he prompted softly. 'I take hold of you and we move together rhythmically.'

This was one game she was never going to win, Kate decided. Nonchalant compliance was the only way if she was to stand a chance of concealing the ridiculous amount of happiness bubbling away inside her at the realisation that he seemed to have forgiven her.

Taking her silence for assent, Guy linked her arm through his and led her towards the patio. Men and women and children were packed in, jostling for space as they danced to the boisterous music. But as soon as they saw Guy approaching some people nudged others and others stopped dancing altogether, until finally the accordionist's fingers faltered and then stilled.

Feeling self-conscious suddenly, Kate pinned an apologetic smile to her face as she glanced around. Perhaps this was as good a moment as any to return to the kitchen.

Sensing her uncertainty, Guy firmed his grip on her arm. '*Continuez*…please,' he insisted. 'Mademoiselle Foster is a little timid…'

'No, I'm not!' Kate whispered fiercely.

He gave a rueful shrug, the corners of his mouth sloping in wry amusement as the music started up again, but at a more sedate pace—and Kate aimed a kick at his shins. 'Missed,' he said, contentedly drawing her close.

With her defiance dispatched at a touch, Kate's senses flared beneath Guy's controlling hands. Firm, but restrained, he left her in no doubt that she would not be allowed to get away until he was ready. Not that she wanted to…ever. But this was only power play for him, she reminded herself forcefully. Guy had always relished the opportunity to bait what he called her wilful spirit—and nothing had changed. She had no doubt he would wield that same power—and with swingeing attention to detail when it came to asserting the wretched covenants when it suited him. But until then… Constraint was seductive, she realised, as the smallest movement of his fingers caused her own to respond, yielding; searching, until the urge to explore the contours of his enclosing fist was impossible to ignore.

Guy made no move either to discourage or encourage, but simply permitted her to twine her fingers through his. It was enough. She was on fire for him. He responded with equal subtlety, one hand shifting very slightly on her waist, increasing the pressure as they moved easily together to the music. His message was unmistakable…if she chose to hear it. Kate flicked a glance around but, having accepted the fact that their Count was happy to mingle with them on the makeshift dance floor, everyone had started dancing again. There was no one to see as she rested her cheek against his chest and wondered what it would be like to have Guy make love to her…to see him focus his mind, his strength and his considerable finesse on pleasuring her.

She could feel the hard contours of his body through the lightweight summer fabrics and picturing him without any clothes on at all didn't take a great leap of the imagination. The thought of Guy stretched out completely naked and fully exposed for her to enjoy on some huge bed was intoxicating. How small she would look next to him, Kate mused, sighing with delicious anticipation as she pressed her breasts up against an unyielding expanse of chest… He would overwhelm her…engulf her with his powerful frame which, if the laws of proportion held true, meant that this wonderful body currently nudging against every erogenous zone she possessed would be completed by the most magnificent erection—the very thought of which sent a bolt of sensation shimmering down her spine to lodge in a place that was already disgracefully receptive. For a moment she could think of nothing at all as she allowed some tantalising little spasms to herald a foretaste of his lovemaking.

She felt his arms tighten around her, almost as if he sensed what was happening, sensed it and supported her so that she could relax into the startlingly pleasurable waves. A moan that was little more than a sigh escaped her as they faded away again far too soon… Hearing that, he stroked one hand very slowly down the length of her back almost as if to console her. She had always known Guy would be a wonderful and intuitive lover; one who knew just how to draw out the pleasure for her until she was forced to beg him for release. He would choose the moment—he would know when to tip her over the edge. He might be all charm, elegance and sophistication on the outside, but those wickedly expressive eyes and all too knowledgeable hands gave him away… They belonged to a connoisseur of the sensual arts, and one who was driving her crazy right now with his whispering passes of a rock-hard thigh against the pulsing site of her arousal.

'Forgive me, Kate… Kate.' He was forced to repeat her

name a little louder to drag her back from her erotic day-dreams.

'Forgive you—' she murmured distractedly, looking up at him with eyes clouded with desire. 'For what?'

'I haven't been paying you enough attention,' he murmured, a gleam of intuition brightening his gaze as he stared down at her.

As his cool minty breath caressed her neck Kate felt all the tiny hairs stand erect. Had he been neglecting her? If this was how it felt to be ignored she couldn't wait to have his full attention. 'Have you been sidetracked? I hadn't noticed.' His eyes were dark with humour when she looked up into them.

'*Bien*, I've been talking to quite a few people,' he said. 'You must have noticed.'

'Well, I didn't,' Kate said, adding by way of an excuse, 'I've been enjoying the dancing too much.'

'So that's what it was,' he said, pretending to be serious, though she could see the amusement tugging at his lips.

'What do you mean?'

'Those little sighs of yours,' he murmured within nibbling distance of her ear.

He seemed to stop just short of exploring it with his tongue and Kate could do nothing to stop the shiver that vibrated through his hands. 'So, what were you talking about?' she said, looking for safer ground.

'Oh, the little personal things that worry people the most.'

'I suppose setting the business back on track has taken up all your time.'

'That's right,' he said. 'And the business must remain a prime concern if it is to flourish. But I think I've turned the corner so it's time to play catch-up on everything I've been missing.'

'Meaning?'

'Meaning, I have time to take a look around at what's

happening closer to home,' he said enigmatically, falling into the rhythm of the slow dance again.

As the darkening sky became tinged with tangerine and magenta their fellow dancers slipped away and it was a moment or two before Kate realised that the music had stopped.

'No, you two, please don't stop on my account—'

As the voice of Guy's mother slipped between Kate and her fantasy, Guy showed no inclination to release her.

'What a lovely party, my dear,' the Countess said, touching her arm. 'We are all so very grateful to you—'

'Oh, no, it was nothing—'

'It was a great deal more than nothing,' the Countess reprimanded her gently. 'You have no idea how it brought people together and made them so happy that all their worries were left behind for an afternoon. Why,' she exclaimed, 'I can't remember anything quite like it since—' She stopped suddenly and Guy reached out his hand. The Countess took it in a firm grip. 'Look at you, you lucky man!' she said, collecting herself hurriedly.

'A beautiful woman on each arm,' he supplied, smiling down at her.

He drew both of them close, planting a kiss on the crown of each head. He would have to make it fair—for the sake of appearances, Kate realised, exchanging smiles with the Countess. 'I'm so pleased you enjoyed yourself. And now you've been to see us, don't be a stranger.'

'Well, actually, that's the reason I wanted to have a word with you,' the Countess said, casting a measuring glance at Kate from beneath a thick fringe of lashes so like her son's.

'Shall we sit down, Mother?' Guy suggested, moving to take her arm.

'Contrary to what you might think, Guy,' she informed him promptly, 'I am quite capable of dancing the night away should I choose to do so.'

'Of course, Mother,' he said, inclining his head in a brief bow.

'Now, Kate,' she said, turning the full beam of still beautiful eyes on Kate's face. 'Megan said it would make more sense if I stayed over at the cottage tonight, and I wanted to speak to you before I agreed. You see,' she continued, seeing Kate's face light up with interest, 'Megan has a plan.'

'A plan?' Guy queried.

'To paint the river at dawn—to capture the special way light filters through the trees… You don't mind?'

'Of course I don't mind, Mother… Kate?'

Kate thought quickly. There was still a very nice guest room going spare, overlooking the garden. 'Of course I don't mind. In fact, I'll probably join you on the painting expedition—'

'Ah…' The Countess looked crestfallen for a moment.

'Is there a problem?' Kate said gently, all her energies focused on nurturing the Countess's tentative return to the outside world.

'My plants—'

'The gardeners can very easily add your prize collection to their watering duties,' Guy pointed out with typical masculine pragmatism.

'Out of the question,' his mother corrected firmly. 'I trust those plants to no one—but Kate. You will do that for me, dear?'

'Of course, but…'

'Last thing at night and first thing in the morning,' the Countess instructed, shooting a warning glance at her son. 'You'll find the feed by the side of the watering can. Guy will show you what to do.' And, having made her wishes clear, she gave Kate's arm a grateful pat then sailed back to join Megan's group of fledgling artists, a group Kate was thrilled to see had grown to include a number of villagers as well as the guests from La Petite Maison.

Realising that either Guy or his chauffeur was now destined to run to and fro with her from the château, Kate turned to offer her apologies.

'I'm very grateful to you for the improvement I see in my mother,' he said bluntly. 'And, frankly, I don't see the problem. Stay over,' he said as if he was inviting her to take tea on the lawn. 'I don't think we should compromise her recovery by placing unnecessary obstacles in her path, do you?'

'Well, no... No, of course not.' Kate's heart stopped. Guy's invitation was so tempting, so full of possibilities. 'But do I really need to stay?' she said, longing for him to insist she did.

'Why not? It's not as if I'm short of bedrooms, and you've stayed at the château before.'

'But it will only take a couple of minutes at most to see to the plants—'

'I thought we had a lot to talk about.'

So much for fantasies! She might have known the covenants would raise their ugly heads sooner or later.

'We might have another drink,' Guy told her reasonably. 'Then I shan't want to drive.'

'But your driver—'

'Will be at Madame Duplessis's disposal.'

Kate thought about it for a moment. Much as she hated being backed into a corner, she could hardly force the issue. 'So, what do you want to discuss?'

'Must I draw up an agenda?'

His choice of words confirmed her suspicions that the topic for discussion was business.

'You've done all you can here,' he pointed out.

Glancing towards the cottage, Kate saw a group of about a dozen people clustered around Megan, hanging on her every word. She needed time to think—to work out how to save the situation. 'But there's the clearing up to do,' she argued.

'Don't you think Madame Duplessis can take care of that?'

Now she saw that a number of staff from the château

had arrived and were setting everything straight again under the housekeeper's direction.

'Let's go,' Guy said, reaching for his jacket.

'I'll need some things—'

'You've got a whole room full of clothes at the château,' he said, drawing her arm through his. 'Or had you forgotten?'

Guy drove his iron-grey Aston Martin straight round to the back of the château and took Kate down the same flight of steps she'd ventured down before. Pausing only to snap on the lights, he led the way across the concrete floor of the vast plant nursery. Opening the door through which he had disappeared on her first visit, he beckoned her in.

'Welcome to Mother's retreat,' he said, bending to switch on a lamp that provided just a mellow glow in contrast to the stark working light they had just left. 'You're very honoured,' he said, stepping deeper into the small room. 'No one is allowed in here apart from me—and now you,' he said, searching her face for a reaction.

Kate stood in silence, looking around, and then turned to shut the door behind her—shutting out the world, she realised, feeling the heavy pall of sadness close around her.

'Perhaps now you can understand why I am so grateful to you,' Guy said softly, leaning back against an old mahogany sideboard housing a collection of beautiful pot plants.

It had seen some wear, Kate thought, though the pictures in their silver frames vying for space amidst the plants had been dusted recently and their frames gleamed bright with attention. There was more furniture in the room—all of it old and shabby, almost as if it had been picked up in one of the characterful flea markets in Paris.

'From their student days,' Guy confirmed, reading her face. 'They shared a small flat—'

'Your mother and father?'

'They were also young once,' he said, his eyes reflecting the depth of his affection for them.

Moving closer, Kate could see the photographs. Some, old and grainy, showed the Countess as a beautiful young girl, her face glowing with vitality…and love. 'Your father was so handsome,' she remarked, seeing the resemblance at once between father and son. She stroked one finger down a lock of ebony hair tied with a white lace ribbon faded in part to yellow that hung over one corner of the frame.

'My father's,' Guy confirmed. 'Taken on honeymoon while he slept and tied with a ribbon Mother saved from her wedding bouquet.'

'That's the most romantic thing I ever heard,' Kate said softly. 'Your mother must have loved him very much.'

'I loved him very much,' Guy corrected gently, 'but he was her life.'

'We must help her,' Kate said passionately as she stared into Guy's eyes. She could see his loss written there as clearly as she had seen it in his mother's eyes, and impulsively she reached out her hand to him. 'I know you're hurting too.'

'We all are,' he said, taking both her hands in his and bringing them to his lips.

'You were right, you know,' Kate admitted.

'About?'

'Me… Aunt Alice. I can see why you were so worried about the way I reacted when the cottage was on fire. This isn't the way…' She gazed about the tiny room filled with a lifetime of memories. 'Thank you.' She watched his eyes grow tender as he looked at her.

'Thank you,' he said softly, leaving go of her hands to take hold of her arms.

'For what?' Kate murmured as a frisson of awareness coursed through her.

'For showing my mother that life can go on,' he said. 'I know it can never be the same again for her, but her recovery is the only memorial my father would ask for. There was a time when I thought this room would become the extent of her world without him—until you came back...'

'Oh, nonsense,' Kate protested softly. 'Megan's the one you should be thanking.' Guy's face told her she was wrong.

'You have no idea how my mother missed you.'

'I missed her too, Guy. And I missed Villeneuve—'

'And me?' he said softly. When she didn't answer, he cupped her face in his hands, making her pulse race as the air between them filled with a heady energy. Dipping his head, Guy brushed his lips very gently against her mouth.

'The plants—' Kate murmured, making no effort to move away.

'Will wait,' Guy said. 'I won't.'

'No, I promised.' But as she went to move away desire curled around the hands she was putting up against his chest and transformed the intended push into a caress.

'Check them, if it makes you feel better.'

He let her go, but Kate could still feel the imprint of his hands. With all the senses in her possession she ached for him. She had waited so long; they both had. She stood for a moment without moving, staring at the plants waiting for her attention and then back again to Guy. She was just as needy as they were, but for Guy's attention—personal and prolonged.

'Go,' he said again softly, dipping his head to urge her across. Their eyes met and locked, like a beam that pulled her towards him rather than away. Seeing her hesitate, he ran one hand lightly down her arm and then up again, keeping hold of her. 'Let's check them together,' he suggested.

Moving slowly down the line, they checked each pot in turn. 'They don't need watering, do they?' Guy said, drawing her round in front of him.

'I don't understand—'

'Like I said,' he whispered against her mouth, 'Mother was young once too.'

*     *     *

It must be a dream, Kate thought as she walked into Guy's private suite of rooms through tall, arched doors. She had never visited this part of the château before, and in contrast to the more public areas it seemed almost Spartan by comparison—yet typically Guy, she thought, gazing around. She saw at once that he'd gone for clean lines, strong shapes and a high degree of comfort. But as he closed the double doors behind them she suddenly felt shy, like a young girl on a first date.

Seeing her face, Guy took her by the hand and brought her with him into the room, switching on some concealed lighting on the way. The floor was square block parquet, the huge windows dressed with sheer drapes. The subtle use of lighting together with a subdued colour palette in shades of white and fawn with touches of yellow ochre gave a sense of order and relaxation. Matching sofas covered in cappuccino suede sat either side of a soft gold wool rug and two large dogs with glossy cinnamon-coloured coats curled around each other in a wicker basket so that it was impossible to tell where one began and the other finished.

'Ric—rac?' Kate queried softly. For as long as she could remember, Guy had kept two dogs—company for each other, he used to say, she remembered with a smile. And as their actions always seemed to mirror each other's, so the single name that split so beautifully into Ric and Rac suited them to perfection—especially as in French their name expressed the boisterous retrievers' penchant for living life by the skin of their teeth.

'Descendants,' he said ruefully as he led her on. 'Time passes.'

Four large wood-framed mirrors drew the eye to a formal group of monochrome shots of impressive office blocks. Seeing her staring at them, Guy stopped and stood behind her with his hands loosely linked around her waist.

'If ever I feel like easing off,' he murmured, nuzzling

against her neck, 'I only have to look at those to remind me how hard I have to work to keep all my companies powering forward.' As she sighed with understanding—or maybe something else—he nudged her hair aside to lavish kisses down her neck.

Kate felt as if she was being enveloped in a seductive cocoon. Guy might be setting a relaxed pace, but they both knew there was only one outcome and that made it the most erotic form of foreplay she could possibly imagine. She was easing into him, melting against him, and had to forcibly drag herself away before she could speak. 'And what about distractions like this?' she demanded softly, turning her face up for his kiss.

'Necessary to life,' he breathed against her mouth.

As she moved in his arms, his hands tracked up slowly from her waist, but before he could claim her breasts Kate broke away with an exclamation. 'What beautiful flowers!' Her curiosity was roused. The bright floral arrangement was the only suggestion of softening in what was essentially a male preserve.

Guy looked at the summer arrangement in the grate of the cream stone fireplace and then back at Kate, his eyes alive with amused speculation as he slanted a look at her.

'Madame Duplessis informed me that my room needed flowers,' he explained.

'Oh.' Relief flooded through her. For a moment she had pictured Guy's mysterious secretary who, in her mind's eye, grew more luscious and irresistible with each passing day. 'Madame Duplessis was right. They are lovely,' Kate managed evenly, 'and they do add something.'

'Oh?'

'Well, your apartment—' She stopped, at a loss for words. It was hardly her place to comment on his unexpectedly contemporary choice of furnishings.

'Isn't what you expected?' Guy supplied. 'But when you have lived all your life surrounded by the splendour of Château Villeneuve, you find that you want very little.

Champagne?' As he spoke he slipped off his jacket and tossed it on to one of the chairs. A smile tugged at the corner of his mouth when he saw her eyes darken.

Collecting herself quickly, Kate tore her glance away from the broad sweep of his shoulders beneath the crisp white shirt and the tantalising glimpse of hard tanned chest shaded with dark hair just visible where he had undone a couple of buttons. 'Were you expecting someone?' she challenged, focusing instead on the ice bucket and glasses.

'Only you,' he said as he loosened his cuffs.

She steeled herself not to look. 'How can I be sure of that?'

'You can't,' he said, rolling back his sleeves.

Kate heard her breathing quicken and grow loud in the silence. There was no way she could ignore the power in his arms, or fail to interpret the look in his eyes. And when he held out his hands to her she went to him without hesitation. He felt so good, so hard and strong, and he tasted as delectable as the warm male scent filling her nostrils. And this time his kiss was not that of an older man respecting the untutored innocence of a much younger woman, but the response of a man meeting his lover on equal terms. He ravished her mouth with a searing hunger, kissing her all the way across the room, backing her towards the door. Then, using one hand to turn the handle, he put his shoulder against it and, swinging her into his arms, carried her across the subtly lit room.

His huge bed was cool and firm, with plump down pillows and an ivory silk throw that he snatched back and threw to the floor. Kate found herself on linen sheets, freshly laundered and scented with lavender. The strength of her passion might have surprised him but he mastered her easily, holding her firm underneath him while he whispered promises that conjured up such erotic images she only begged him for more and in words she barely recognised.

But Guy was too strong for her and would not be hurried.

He chose instead to watch her responses with a lazy interest, capturing her wrists and holding them high above her head whilst tracing an unhurried path down her neck, her shoulder and then her arm with his other hand. Time was suspended in a realm where sensation ruled and Kate barely registered the fact that he had eased the zip down the back of her dress until she felt him teasing her nipple with his tongue through the taut lace of her bra.

With long, shuddering sighs, she meshed her fingers through his thick black hair, increasing the pressure, but he broke away, taking his shirt over his head in one fluid move. As he reached for the buckle on his black leather belt she watched him release it, thrilling with pleasure to see him as eager as she was to be rid of his clothes. Then, as he lowered the zip on his linen trousers and swung off the bed to step out of them, she feasted her eyes again on his iron-flat stomach banded with muscle. Relishing her female power, Kate allowed her gaze to rove slowly and appreciatively over his magnificently proportioned torso and then on to where his black silk underpants accentuated, rather than concealed, his raging desire. Sprawling back with one arm tucked comfortably behind her head, she bent one knee a little, deliberately and very provocatively, as she continued to stare at him.

Realising he was the floor show with an audience of one, Guy caught her gaze and returned it loaded with the promise of delicious retribution. Then, matching his length to hers, he rested his head on the heel of his hand and scorched a trail with his eyes over every deeply aroused inch of her. Only after what seemed like the longest time did he turn his attention back to her face. 'Your lips are red and swollen from my kisses,' he observed, tracing them with one firm thumb pad. 'Your eyes are emerald-bright and feverish with desire… And your hair is gloriously disordered and streaming over your breasts…'

Each of his words was like a caress and each one of them stimulated her a little more. She gasped out loud when his hand claimed her breast. But when she reached for him he only laughed softly and held her hand away.

'Not yet,' he said, scoring tantalising circles around her achingly sensitive nipples with the tips of his nails. 'Take your bra off for me first.' And now it was his turn to settle back to watch her with his head resting comfortably on his arms.

'Not yet,' Kate said, deliberately provoking him. Straddling him so that she had the comfort of feeling his arousal against her, she thrust out her breasts. She knew how Guy loved to toy with her responses, play her effortlessly so that as each moment passed she thought the next would bring satisfaction, only to have him deny her again... Well, now it was her turn. As he moved forward to take matters into his own hands she leaned back. 'Not yet,' she repeated in a voice full of irony.

But she had underestimated him and his reflexes were lightning-fast. The gasp as he swung her underneath him turned to a moan as his hands closed over each distended nipple and his thumbs began to chafe them firmly, mercilessly through the taut fabric until the livid buds became unbearably sensitive. 'You always did like playing games,' he said. 'Is this what you had in mind?'

'Yes... Oh, yes—' she managed before his plundering mouth cut her off again. And then her bra was gone and her lush breasts were fully exposed for his perusal. She had the satisfaction of hearing his sharp breath of approval before strong hands robbed her mind of the power of thought as they moved to measure and stroke and clasp and mould. Then, dipping his head to suckle, he teased her with his lips and with his teeth until she knew she would go mad with frustration.

As she sucked in a deep and shuddering breath he looked up, but the confident humour in his eyes warned her that he hadn't finished with her yet. Teasing her breasts with his hands, he lit a trail of fire down to her waist with his kisses until, finally easing her thighs apart, he sank down between her legs.

He nuzzled the damp scrap of lace, tracing the swollen lips it confined with his tongue. But as Kate lifted her knees and cupped her hands behind them, opening herself more for his enjoyment, with a low growl of triumph he seized the thong and ripped it off. Kate responded immediately, impatient fingers slipping beneath the waistband of his black silk underwear. Guy allowed her to wrestle him for a while until, pushing her on to her back, he brought the playfulness to a close with stroking fingers and a mouth that knew too much about pleasure. But when almost immediately Kate found herself teetering on the edge of release she tried to push him away.

Lifting his head, he murmured wryly, 'This is no time to be self-conscious.'

'I know,' Kate admitted huskily, turning her head away to mumble, 'but I'm scared.'

Reaching a hand up, he cupped her chin to turn her back to face him. 'Scared of what, baby…losing control?' And when she didn't answer he coaxed her legs apart again. 'Don't worry… I've got you. Let go.'

And when she did as he said it was with such a burst of sensation she cried out in astonishment and bucked against him for the longest time until he wrapped her tightly in his arms and kissed her more intimately and more tenderly than ever before. 'And now it's my turn,' he murmured, guiding her hand down to where there was no hope at all of containing him within one of her fine-boned fists. But when the fears came back he knew just how to soothe them and how to tempt her on until, lodging one powerful thigh between her legs, he finally held her powerless beneath him.

'I'm really frightened now,' Kate admitted in a gasp, and more by his size than any doubt as to his consideration for her.

'No, you're not,' Guy insisted huskily, warming her ear with his breath. 'You're inexperienced and apprehensive, but never frightened, Kate—not with me. I would never, never hurt you.'

With her gaze firmly locked in his she accepted the steady thrust, trusting him completely as he stretched her beyond anything she would have thought possible, filling her with an intensity of sensation she could never have anticipated. The sense of completeness made her cry out his name and she stabbed her fingers into his taut buttocks as he withdrew slowly, making him plunge deeply again. And as he felt her rise towards him in an unmistakable plea for more Guy built the rhythm, adding a little more force each time until they were moving urgently together.

He was supremely responsive, moving with firm, deep strokes to inflame the quiver within her until it became an all-consuming need, and when the pulsating energy consumed them both the violence of his spasms prolonged her own stunning release. For a while it seemed to Kate as if the aftershocks would never end. But Guy knew just how to soothe her back down again, tucking strands of damp hair behind her ears and bathing her face with kisses, then stroking her body until finally she quietened against him and snuggled contentedly into the nook between his neck and shoulder.

'No sleep,' he warned softly. 'Not yet.'

'Why not?' she said faintly in a sleep-slurred voice.

'Because,' he murmured, moving on to his side, 'I'm not finished with you yet.'

'Oh, really?' Kate breathed as she stretched out languorously with her arms flung up to rest on the soft mound of pillows.

'Yes, really,' Guy insisted in a voice laced with dry humour as he moved one of her legs over his thighs, spreading her wide again.

As he settled in closer Kate felt him brush against her as he turned her on to her side. And this time when he thrust inside her there was no fear, only moans of sheer delight as he proved she still needed his attention. 'Are you never satisfied?' she gasped as he took up the familiar rhythm and intensified the sensation with the steady movement of his fingers.

'I just want to make sure you don't forget me while I'm away,' he said as he used the heel of one hand to nudge her into the best position.

'Away?'

But this was not the time for discussion, and Guy made sure that pleasure took her over until the thought that he might be leaving soon was submerged beneath tidal waves of sensation.

Kate woke to find Guy dressed ready to go out. The dark formal suit, together with the tailored shirt and silk tie instantly rang warning bells in her mind. 'Where are you going?' she said, suddenly wide awake. As he bent to plant a kiss on her mouth she sat up and they clashed with an awkwardness totally at odds with the harmony they had enjoyed only hours before.

'I'm sorry,' he said softly as he straightened up. 'I didn't mean to wake you. Something urgent's cropped up—business,' he explained reassuringly when he saw the look on her face. 'Don't worry, I won't be away long. Go back to sleep.'

His voice was soothing, and maybe he stayed until she went back to sleep, or maybe she simply never woke up properly in the first place, Kate thought drowsily when she woke up later that same morning. But Guy had said nothing about going away, she thought, tossing back the covers. A pang of uncertainty hit her square in the stomach. They hadn't exactly had a proper conversation, she remembered as she sat up. Torrid images hit her all together, blotting out the tenderness and leaving doubt in its place. This just wasn't like her, Kate realised, clutching her knees as she struggled to hang on to the fact that she was rational, sensible and cautious by nature and that Guy was the most honourable man she knew. No, she argued with herself as she buried her face. That was how she used to be, until Guy turned her whole world on its head—and he had only taken what was freely offered.

Why should he tell her where he was going? What hold did she have on him? Had last night meant nothing to him? She felt physically sick as she bit down hard on her lip and tried not to care. The trouble was she loved him; she had always loved him and always would love him. And what if he didn't feel the same? She cast about in desperation for some strong independent woman theme to provide her with a survival strategy, but it didn't work. She knew she would take whatever Guy had to give her and on whatever terms he chose.

# CHAPTER NINE

'WHAT do you mean, the electricity is off again?' Kate asked Megan as soon as she arrived back at La Petite Maison. 'Guy's only just had it reconnected.'

'Some snip of a woman turned up with a clipboard under her arm and a sheaf of papers under her arm. These are for you,' Megan said grimly, handing Kate a package. 'Where is his Lordship?' she said, scarcely pausing for breath. 'You might need him.'

'Guy?' Kate said distractedly as she headed for the kitchen table. 'He had an urgent business meeting.' Already she felt as if they had been apart for a lifetime—even a moment without him was too long.

'At the château?' Megan said, breaking into her thoughts.

'I don't know where he's gone,' Kate admitted, suddenly feeling very unsure of herself.

'You did discuss the guest house with him?' Megan said confidently.

'No,' Kate said uncomfortably. 'I'm sorry, Megan, but we just never got round to it. I saw to the plants and then went to bed and...' Her voice tailed away. She was no better than Megan was at telling lies. 'What's wrong?'

'I'm afraid you won't find our next batch of guests half as accommodating as the last if their e-mails are anything to go by,' Megan said, looking anxiously over Kate's shoulder while she emptied the documents from the foolscap envelope on to the table. 'And I'd bet a pound to a penny that this isn't good news either,' she added ominously.

'Where is everyone?' Kate said, realising the cottage was very quiet as she focused on the first page.

'With the Countess at the château,' Megan explained,

cheering up a little. 'She invited everyone to take a tour of the gardens. That young chauffeur of hers came for them in a mini-bus.'

'That young chauffeur,' Kate echoed wryly, relishing the moment of distraction. But soon she was frowning again as she skimmed through the sheaf of papers. 'But these are yet more translations of the covenants,' she said, 'and a covering letter that says if we continue to trade as a guest house the Villeneuve estate will close us down.' Badly shaken, she dropped the whole lot on the table in disgust. Had Guy orchestrated this little surprise for her, knowing he would be well out of the way when the bombshell struck? Or could it be someone working independently— someone with much to gain, seizing the moment while he was away?

'They're not the translations you're paying for, are they?' Megan asked anxiously, cutting into her cogitations.

'No, of course not,' Kate confirmed. 'I'll only have sight of those when my solicitor returns from holiday.'

'So these could be any old tripe and onions,' Megan proclaimed contemptuously. 'It's not as if they were even delivered by Guy. He probably knows nothing about them.'

'How can I be sure of that?' Kate said, as the fear that Guy had betrayed her reared up and demanded a hearing.

'You can't be sure of anything until you speak to him,' Megan pointed out sensibly. 'You know his mother loves the idea of you having the guest house here. And you said it yourself—he was grateful for the part our activities are playing in her recovery.'

'He didn't say that exactly,' Kate said. 'He just guessed what we were up to and decided to turn a blind eye—for the duration of the party, at least. I'm not sure he would approve if we turn La Petite Maison into a full-time business.'

'All right, then.' Megan dismissed the licence she'd

taken with a theatrical gesture. 'So, all you need to do now is talk to him, Kate—'

'If only life was that simple.'

'But it is that simple, if you'll only slow down and allow it to be,' Megan said with her usual self-assurance.

'Just because the Countess has decided to involve herself with such enthusiasm doesn't mean Guy can be persuaded to do the same,' Kate said. 'You're a hopeless romantic, Megan,' she scolded gently. 'Why would Guy have sent another set of documents over if he supported our venture?'

'Who says he sent them over?'

'This woman, presumably.'

'Huh!'

'He's had plenty of opportunity to talk to me about it, but he chose not to,' Kate said, trying to reason with an entirely adamant Megan.

'Maybe he had other things on his mind,' Megan murmured, pretending interest in some paintbrushes she had soaking in jars by the sink. 'So, Kate,' she said, swinging round with her hands planted firmly on her hips, 'if his Lordship's gone walkabout, what are you going to do about our little problem?'

Kate squared her shoulders as she made her decision. 'Tell me about this woman.'

'Blonde, beautiful, thirtyish,' Megan said, screwing up her face as she thought about it. 'With all the charm of a white shark hunting.'

'You liked her?' Kate suggested wryly to mask her concern.

'She seemed pretty sure of herself,' Megan observed, her lips pursing in a tight, disapproving grimace. 'Who do you think she was?'

'I've no idea,' Kate admitted edgily. 'Estate manager, perhaps?'

'You'll find a solution. You always have before,' Megan asserted confidently.

Maybe not this time, Kate thought. Maybe this time she had slipped up badly, and not just on the business front. But for now there was no point getting Megan all worked up. 'I'll take a shower and then I'll get straight round to the estate office,' she said, throwing herself into work mode.

After a quick shower, Kate telephoned the Villeneuve estate office and was eventually put through to the woman she had spoken to before. The woman she had always supposed was Guy's secretary.

'Mariamme D'Arbo, can I help you?' The voice was lightly accented and sounded impatient even before Kate had a chance to state her reason for calling.

'This is Kate Foster,' Kate said in a pleasant enough voice that stopped short of encouraging pointless civilities.

'Ah, Mademoiselle Foster—' The voice had hardened considerably now. 'I take it you have read the documents I brought round to the cottage? I hand-carried them to ensure that they arrived safely.'

Kate had no intention of being patronised and surmised that the woman also had taken the opportunity to have a good look around. And poor Megan would scarcely have been on her guard... She might have thought the woman was a prospective guest. Deciding to take no chances, Kate proceeded cautiously but firmly. 'As Monsieur le Compte is out of the country,' she said, 'I would like to arrange an immediate appointment to speak to whoever is in charge while he is away.'

Seconds ticked until she was on the point of asking if Mariamme D'Arbo was still there, when the other woman spoke. 'That would be me, *mademoiselle*.'

She sounded amused—and smug. Without missing a beat, Kate came back, 'In that case, I'd like to make an appointment to see you.' But the cogs in her mind were whirring off the scale. Who the hell was this woman?

'That may not be possible, *mademoiselle*. I am very busy for the next couple of weeks, as you can imagine—'

'Make time,' Kate said coolly, reverting to business mode. 'You can't just serve eviction papers and then refuse point-blank to discuss them.'

A few moments passed and then she was informed in a bored voice, 'I may be able to shuffle things around. I shall have to consult my diary.'

'I'll wait,' Kate said. There was a great deal of paper-rustling at the other end of the line but Kate would have bet La Petite Maison that it was a pointless display made solely for effect.

'No, *mademoiselle*,' the weary voice came back to her at last. 'It is just as I told you before. I regret—'

'I shall be at your office at nine o'clock tomorrow morning,' Kate said firmly. 'I take it you will be in at nine? I shan't take up much of your time. Goodbye, Ms D'Arbo.'

Slamming the phone down, she held it down almost as if Mariamme D'Arbo might be capable of anything, even transmitting her unpleasantness through the cable. The next call Kate made was to her solicitor in England, but he was still out of the office. She briefly considered phoning Guy, but if he was on her side she had nothing to worry about and should get on with sorting out the problem herself, and if he wasn't—well, in that case, she had no option but to do exactly the same thing. And then she realised that she didn't even have his mobile number and started worrying all over again.

'Have you sorted it out yet?' Megan asked, as if reading Kate's mind. Leaning her considerable bulk against the table, she surveyed Kate, a concerned frown playing across her homely features.

'Not yet,' Kate admitted. 'But I have made an appointment to see the woman who brought the papers round.'

'Wouldn't I like to be a fly on the wall when that confrontation takes place,' Megan commented wryly.

'It's just as well you won't be,' Kate said. 'I can't imagine it will make for relaxing viewing.'

'Just as I'd hoped,' Megan said with a wink as she scooped up her paintbrushes. 'Ah, well, I'd better be setting up for this evening's art classes—'

'Light through the trees by the river at sunset, perchance?' Kate suggested dryly.

'Don't you go playing little Miss Innocent with me,' Megan advised, giving Kate a shrewd look. 'You can't tell me that the Countess and I didn't find the perfect excuse to give you and Guy some time together?'

Perhaps it would have been better if they hadn't, Kate thought, feeling vulnerable again. 'I should have joined you when I said I would,' she murmured half to herself.

'You'll feel differently when Guy comes back,' Megan said with great confidence as she headed for the door.

Another stab of anxiety pierced Kate's heart. 'I hope you're right,' she said softly.

'Why don't you ring him? Put your mind at ease?'

Sweet, pragmatic Megan… Of course she should ring him. If they had thought to exchange numbers it might have helped! But why should they when Guy had given not the slightest indication that anything would change at Villeneuve while he was away? He was either totally unscrupulous or completely unaware of what was going on, Kate realised unhappily. Either way she was on her own.

'I can handle this perfectly well without Guy's help,' she insisted, assuming an air of confidence she didn't feel. Megan's facial expression was hardly encouraging. 'What?' Kate demanded. 'Do you think this woman is not all she seems?'

'I don't know who, or what, she is,' Megan said disparagingly. 'But I do know I don't like her. Just be careful, Kate.'

'Don't worry, Megan. I didn't invite you to join me in this enterprise only to lose everything without putting up a fight. And I have no intention of taking any risks either,' Kate promised. 'There's too much at stake here—for all of us.'

'What then?'

'Initially…' Kate pondered for a moment. 'I'll kill her with kindness—throw myself on her mercy—whatever it takes, but I have to play for time until I can work out who she is, how far her authority can take her and how to hold her off until I've spoken to Guy.'

Mademoiselle D'Arbo had a body to die for, the face of an angel and, Megan was right, all the hunting instincts of a shark, Kate decided within the first few seconds. She had also turned up for their meeting in business uniform consisting of a tailored suit and an immaculately cut white shirt. But there was one interesting accessory, Kate thought, viewing the enormous sapphire and diamond ring she wore on the fourth finger of her left hand. Ignoring the stab of concern that it could have anything to do with Guy, Kate squared her shoulders and confronted the coldest pair of blue eyes she had ever seen in her life.

'I'm surprised Monsieur le Comte didn't think to mention his intention to push forward the enforcement of the covenants before he left on business,' she said mildly, waiting to gauge the response of her adversary.

'Perhaps he only decided to take action after seeing you—and before speaking to me,' Mariamme D'Arbo replied smugly.

Smooth…very smooth, Kate decided as she watched the other woman settle herself back in the chair. 'I think there's been a mistake,' Kate continued calmly. 'But I'm sure we can work something out. There has to be a reasonable compromise that will satisfy both parties.'

'I think the Villeneuve estate has been more than reasonable with you, Miss Foster,' Mariamme D'Arbo said coldly. 'Le Comte de Villeneuve expects this matter to be settled before he returns.' Picking up an envelope from the desk, she passed it to Kate.

'What's this?'

'Why don't you open it and see?'

Keeping her gaze fixed on Mariamme D'Arbo's face, Kate ripped open the envelope and extracted several thin slips of paper. Bills for repairs, she read, her eyes widening as she looked through the list. The total amount was colossal, and when she looked at the payment details she saw that Guy seemed to be using an offshore bank—

'And, once that is settled, the Villeneuve estate demands your immediate surrender of the property—'

'You're evicting me?'

'That is correct. And with immediate effect.'

'On whose authority?' Kate demanded icily.

'Mine—my partner's…'

Kate didn't hear any more as she sprang to her feet. It had never occurred to her that Guy might have a partner. And she was pretty sure that this woman was the same person she had spoken to on the phone—the young woman she had imagined was his secretary. Kate's stomach lurched as she wondered if she had made a classic mistake—a mistake that was generally the preserve of the male of the species—a mistake she should have been the very last person on earth to be guilty of making. She glanced again at the payment terms on the invoice.

'I'll need to check the details on this invoice against my records. I assume I have the usual twenty-eight days' credit—'

'Payment is due immediately,' Mariamme D'Arbo informed her bluntly. 'Some of this work was completed weeks ago, and one thing I have noticed since I came here is how lax the accounts department has become—'

'Really?' Kate said coolly. 'Have you been working here long?' Since Guy had taken over the word was his accounts department was one of the best.

'Long enough,' Mariamme D'Arbo said as she stood up. 'Now, if you'll excuse me, I'm very busy—'

'You should know that no amount of money could persuade me to leave La Petite Maison, Ms D'Arbo,' Kate cut in firmly. 'I am totally committed to completing the restoration of the cottage. You must understand—'

'No,' the other woman spat before Kate had chance to finish, 'I'm afraid I don't understand.'

'Nevertheless, it is a fact,' Kate said pleasantly. 'So I shan't be making any plans to leave the cottage, or pay this bill, until I have spoken to the Count.'

Mariamme D'Arbo had clearly been expecting an easy ride. Dealing with Kate was not what she had been expecting at all. 'Well, the electricity won't be turned back on,' she announced. 'And if you don't pay, we'll sue. As for arranging a meeting with the Count—' She shrugged dismissively, as if a meeting with Guy would serve no purpose whatever.

'I've managed without electricity before,' Kate said, managing to sound calm even though her heart was dancing a fandango at the thought of how her next guests might react. From what Megan had told her, she was pretty sure primitive conditions didn't figure in their holiday plans. 'And, as for suing me—' She shrugged.

'You will find that the Count agrees with me on the matter of covenants,' Mariamme D'Arbo cut in. 'And I know that we both have the same thoughts on holiday cottages cluttering up the estate—let alone boarding houses.'

The way Marianne D'Arbo linked herself with Guy was the last straw as far as Kate was concerned. 'Boarding houses?' she returned icily. 'I know of no boarding houses on the Villeneuve estate.'

'Oh, come now, Miss Foster. Do you mean to tell me that La Petite Maison could be described in any other way?'

The urge to screw up the documents into bite-sized balls and make her eat them was overwhelming, Kate realised, as she hung on for grim death to what remained of her self-control. 'I'm not sure the Count would agree with your views,' she argued firmly, and had the satisfaction of seeing just a glimmer of unease appear in the stony blue eyes. 'So, why don't we give him the opportunity to express his own opinions?' she suggested as she got up. Extending her hand, she added coolly, 'Perhaps you'll ring me if you hear anything from him before I do, Mademoiselle D'Arbo? I'll jot my number down on this pad for you— to ensure you have it,' she added with a nice touch of irony.

Mariamme D'Arbo's stare was like a blade that longed to cut Kate off at the knees and make her grovel. But that wasn't about to happen, and neither was she going to demean herself by asking for Guy's telephone number, Kate decided, holding her head up high as she sailed out of the room. 'Goodbye, Ms D'Arbo,' she called over her shoulder.

The light of battle was still in Kate's eyes when she arrived back at the cottage, but she had a cookery class straight after lunch and it was almost a relief to put all her energies into preparing for that. She was halfway through laying out ingredients in separate piles for each guest when her mobile rang.

'Guy? Guy!' There was too much static to hear anything clearly but her thundering heart told her who it was. Then the line cut abruptly. Nursing the phone like a baby, Kate paced up and down the kitchen, realising how much she wanted him back... At least face-to-face she might hope to reason with him—to point out what a sinister secretary, partner, or whatever he chose to call her, he had left to mind the shop while he was away. Her mind was on fire with all the reasons why he should get rid of the woman. She almost dropped the telephone when it rang again. 'Guy... Where are you? How did you get my number? The line's terrible.'

'Stop talking,' he said crisply. 'Just tell me, are you all right?'

'Of course I'm all right.' The concern in his voice frightened her.

'Only—'

'Guy! Guy!' Kate gusted with impatience as the persistent crackling drowned him out. 'Give me your number at least—' But the line had cut again and, glancing out of the window, she saw that her guests had arrived back from the château. Whatever Guy had been trying to tell her would have to wait.

Trying to ignore the shiver of apprehension his call had provoked, she turned her attention to the colourful group clambering out of the mini-bus. Their faces were glowing from exposure to the warm summer sunshine and something else, Kate thought. It wasn't too extravagant to say they had been transformed since their arrival at La Petite Maison. There was camaraderie and an energy that had been lacking when they had arrived. For a moment she envied them. They had all found something very special to take home with them.

'Uh,' Megan huffed as she exploded into the kitchen with her usual gusto. 'What a great time we've had!' Grinning from ear to ear, she slapped down her multi-coloured tasselled bag on the table, adding, 'But I'm totally bushed.'

Kate took the hint. 'Don't worry,' she said. 'I'll take over now. And there's some freshly squeezed orange juice in the cooler. Let me get you some.' As she hurried to get glasses for everyone she realised that she had never been more grateful to Megan and their guests. As the kitchen filled with excited chatter, the elation was just what she needed to feed on. She could feel her energy levels rising by the minute.

'We went through the maze at the château,' one of the elderly ladies revealed with a shy smile as she helped Kate to hand round the drinks.

'Some of us more quickly than others,' Dirk, the retired

rocker from Bermondsey, admitted ruefully, running bony fingers through what remained of his straggly hair.

'Well, at least you all came through,' Kate said warmly. 'That's quite an achievement. I remember getting lost there many times—'

'On purpose, we always suspected,' Megan confided to everyone cheerfully. 'There was only one person who knew every twist and turn and that was the young Count de Villeneuve. So it was a very good way to get his attention. Isn't that right, Kate?'

'I couldn't possibly comment,' Kate said, wondering if her heart would always caper round her chest at the sound of Guy's name. And she hadn't fooled Megan or Aunt Alice…and if they had known what she was up to, then Guy would have done too… Which zigzag route brought her back to wondering where he was and when he'd return—

'You haven't heard from Guy yet?' Megan murmured, seeing the concern on her face.

Shaking her head, Kate couldn't help wondering why he hadn't rung back. There had been real tension in his voice. Had he been trying to warn her of something? Or was he simply checking up on her? There was so much she needed to ask him…about Mariamme D'Arbo, mostly. Should she follow her head and conclude that Ms D'Arbo was Guy's business partner as well as— She drew herself up short. She couldn't even bear to think about any other possibility. She knew it was the wrong time to be mulling over personal matters… Why couldn't she just believe in Guy, as she always had?

'It's a matter of trust,' she blurted out, as if her thoughts were too tumultuous to be contained. And when everyone turned to look at her, she added quickly, 'The maze, I mean… Trust takes time to build—years maybe under normal circumstances…' She glanced around helplessly. 'What I'm trying to say is that you've all come to trust each other in the space of just a few days. That's good, isn't it?'

'Bravo!' Megan said, coming to her rescue with a round of applause. 'Where would we be without trust, eh?' she demanded, staring round the group.

'With it we'll all be back here again next year,' Dirk ventured, looking hopefully round at his newfound friends for confirmation.

Kate was touched by Dirk's diffident endorsement of her dream and was relieved when a chorus of agreement met his declaration. It was all she needed to shunt her own concerns on to a siding. This was the group's last night and she was determined to make it a good one for them. And, as she handed round some aromatic ginger cake, she couldn't help thinking that without trust she might have been left wondering whether to believe Mariamme D'Arbo or Guy.

Late that same evening Kate was alone in the kitchen when the Countess de Villeneuve arrived. Alone and on foot and in a terrible state, Guy's mother practically fell into her arms when Kate opened the door. 'Countess, what's happened?' Kate exclaimed as she drew her inside.

'That woman,' she managed breathlessly, leaning on Kate's arm as Kate led her across the room to settle her into what had quickly become her favourite spot by the old range.

Kate didn't need to ask to whom the Countess was referring, and simply poured a large measure of good brandy into a cut-glass goblet and handed it to her.

'She's saying the most terrible things,' the Countess gasped out between sips.

'Slow down, take some deep breaths,' Kate encouraged soothingly, 'and then try and tell me what's happened.'

'I couldn't stay there,' the Countess continued, her voice shaking with emotion. 'I couldn't watch her making herself comfortable in my home. Not after the terrible things she said. I had to come here to you. I hope I've done the right thing—'

'Of course you have. But surely you can't mean that Mariamme D'Arbo has moved into the château?'

The Countess could only nod dumbly. 'She took my engagement ring,' she managed finally, turning agonised eyes on Kate's face.

'Sapphire and diamond?' The red-rimmed eyes locked on to her face told her all she needed to know. 'Don't worry. I promise I'll get it back for you,' Kate said, fired with a determination that no amount of bullying by Ms D'Arbo was going to deflate.

'That's not all,' the Countess admitted haltingly.

'Tell me,' Kate said, kneeling down by her side.

'I shouldn't trouble you with this, but—'

'Don't say that,' Kate said, covering her hands with her own. 'You did exactly the right thing coming to me.'

The Countess shook her head in helpless despair. 'I needed somewhere peaceful... Somewhere where I could try and digest all the scandalous things she said.'

'What scandalous things? What has she said to hurt you so much?'

She said...' The Countess pressed her lips together as if it was too much for her to express what she had learned in words.

'Go on,' Kate urged softly, taking both the Countess's thin, veined hands between her own. 'I know who you're talking about. I've met her. So there's nothing you can say that can possibly surprise me.'

'Then you know, Kate, how hard she is—how pitiless...'

'I know how calculating—how driven she is. But I also know that she's just a bully. She can't do us any real harm—'

'No!' the Countess exclaimed. 'You're wrong—'

'Why don't we just call the police? We can do it now,'

Kate said, glancing towards the telephone. 'That woman has no right to move into the château—'

'No. You don't understand, Kate. It seems she has every right. She can do so much harm to all of us… You have no idea—'

'Tell me everything,' Kate insisted calmly. 'Then I can start to put your mind at rest.'

'All right.' The Countess took a long, shuddering breath. 'She says she is the illegitimate daughter of my late husband, Guy's father—'

'What?'

'And she says Guy has no option but to make her his partner—' Her voice wobbled and then broke into uncontrollable sobs.

At that moment Kate could cheerfully have thrown Mariamme D'Arbo bodily out of Villeneuve for the harm she had done, but instead she reached for some kitchen towel and asked quietly, 'Has she given you any proof of this?'

Guy's mother shook her head vigorously. 'Can you believe how cruel she is? Suggesting that Raoul could father a child when I know that we never spent a single night apart from the day we were married?'

'But that's your answer,' Kate pointed out gently. 'She's done a terrible thing, cruel beyond belief. But you know the truth. And somehow we're going to prove that you're right and that this woman is nothing but a cheap impostor.'

'But how, Kate… How?' the Countess keened as she rocked back and forth. 'She's terrorising everyone at the château—'

'Not Madame Duplessis,' Kate said confidently.

'No, but until Guy returns no one's sure what to believe. Without clear leadership they're afraid to act.'

Kate knew she had no authority to start throwing her weight around… She would just have to be as cunning as her opponent.

'Do you think you could do something?' the Countess said, as if reading her mind.

'I'm not sure yet,' Kate admitted honestly. 'But I don't think we can afford to wait for Guy to return. Who knows what else she might steal?'

'There's more,' the Countess confessed.

'I need to know everything,' Kate prompted.

The Countess nodded agreement, mopping her eyes again before she continued in a stronger voice. 'She says that she has proof that you have contravened the covenants and that she has full authority to repossess La Petite Maison. She wants me to sign some document—'

'You haven't?' Kate said quickly.

'That's why I came here—to get away from her.'

'Good,' Kate said with a sigh of relief.

'But she says she can take over the business if she gets proof that Guy knows about your...your... Oh, I'm so sorry, Kate. Your business enterprise,' she said finally, as if she couldn't bear to lay any blame at Kate's door.

'Hold on,' Kate said, catching hold of the Countess's flailing hands. 'Let's look at this logically. Why has she waited until now to show herself? Why not seek out your husband during his lifetime?'

The Countess leaned forward, her eyes wide as she confided hoarsely, 'She says it has taken her up to now to get all her ducks in a row.'

From the way the Countess spoke, as if gathering all the threads of her memory together to make quite sure she got it right, Kate gathered that this was a direct quote. 'I bet it has,' she said coolly. 'Have you managed to speak to Guy at all?'

'No, Kate. Have you?'

'I think Ms D'Arbo chose her time well. For some reason, Guy's had trouble using his mobile, or I know he'd have been in touch long before now.'

'Do you think someone's got to it?' the Countess said

tensely, clearly relishing the crime novel idiom now that Kate had given her some hope. 'He won't stop to use a public telephone if he even suspects there's a problem here. I know Guy. He'll drive through the night—'

'Actually, I think that's entirely possible,' Kate confirmed. 'There's a lot at stake, and I don't imagine Mariamme D'Arbo is working alone. I couldn't trace his number back when he called me... But he may be on his way home right now,' she mused softly.

'Oh, do you really think so?' the Countess said eagerly.

'Wherever he is, it's up to me to stop Mademoiselle D'Arbo doing any more damage.'

'Do you think you can?'

'I know I can,' Kate replied with steely determination. 'But for now, Countess,' she said softly, training her steady gaze on the old lady's darting eyes, 'why don't you stay over here tonight? Get some sleep. We'll tackle this together in the morning.'

'You make it sound so tempting,' the Countess said wistfully. 'I'd love to, but what about Madame Duplessis? She must be so worried about me.'

'Leave Madame Duplessis to me,' Kate said reassuringly. 'I need to speak to her in any event.'

'Well, if you're quite sure.'

'I am,' Kate confirmed, helping Guy's mother out of the chair. 'Go to bed,' she insisted softly, leaning over to plant a kiss on the old lady's paper-dry cheek. 'I always keep the room you used before ready for you—just in case,' she said with a smile. 'And you should know by now that worries aren't given house room here at La Petite Maison.' Kate watched the Countess's shoulders relax as she turned one last trusting look on her face before mounting the stairs.

Once she was sure her elderly charge was properly reassured, Kate walked over to the telephone and began to dial. As she had known she would be, Madame Duplessis was most co-operative, even more so in light of the fact that Mariamme D'Arbo was already encroaching on the housekeeper's territory.

'And she's wearing all those beautiful clothes that the Count bought for you,' Madame Duplessis said in a tone as close to outrage as years of control and good manners allowed.

'Never mind the clothes,' Kate said, almost amused for a moment by the fact that something so trivial could engage the housekeeper's attention when there was so much at stake. 'Can you do what I ask?'

'But of course, Mademoiselle Foster. It would be my pleasure.'

'Good. I'll call round for the package first thing in the morning—before anyone is awake.'

'I quite understand, *mademoiselle*,' Madame Duplessis confirmed briskly. 'I shall be waiting for you at the rear entrance of the west wing at dawn.'

Having set her scheme in motion, Kate wrote a brief note to Megan, alerting her to the fact that the Countess was staying the night and asking her to say farewell to their guests. Fortunately, as this group had arrived a few days early, there would be a lull now until the next group arrived.

Kate hardly slept at all that night. She was sure now that Mariamme D'Arbo was nothing more than a confidence trickster, a woman whose sole motive in coming to Villeneuve was to plunder as much as she could whilst Guy was away. That certainty, together with the conviction that this was Ms D'Arbo's day of reckoning, ensured that she was up, dressed and out of the cottage as the first silvery strands of daylight stole across the night sky.

The hand-over was quick and silent. Pocketing the sealed polythene package, Kate jumped back into her car and headed straight for the village. Monsieur Dupont was already standing outside the *pharmacie*, staring up the road in the direction he knew she would be coming.

'My brother is waiting for us at the laboratory,' he said as he climbed in beside her. 'Do you have everything he requires?'

'I do,' Kate confirmed, feeling like an agent in a spy thriller as she handed over the package. 'Madame Duplessis has labelled the evidence for him.'

'Hair, I believe you said?' Monsieur Dupont enquired, holding the package up and squinting at it in the rapidly increasing light.

'That's correct,' Kate said, smiling to herself. 'A strand of the late Count's hair and a collection of hairs from Mademoiselle D'Arbo's hairbrush.'

'Perfect,' Monsieur Dupont declared with satisfaction. 'We shall unmask the impostor with a simple DNA test and set everyone's mind at rest.'

'I only hope you're right,' Kate said, putting her foot down on the accelerator pedal.

'I can assure you, Mademoiselle Foster, I am never wrong,' Monsieur Dupont proclaimed with his customary assurance.

Kate smiled through her exhaustion as she thumped her pillows into submission. Monsieur Dupont had been proved correct and, thanks to his brother, the DNA results had come through quickly, proving beyond doubt that Mariamme D'Arbo was a fraud. She had been escorted off the Villeneuve estate and was now being questioned by the local police, with Interpol waiting in the wings.

Kate knew her loyalties had changed irrevocably after everything that had happened. Villeneuve and everyone connected with it had a far greater hold on her than ever. Even her position as Chief Executive of Freedom Holidays paled by comparison. The look on Comtesse de Villeneuve's face when she had received irrefutable proof that her late husband had been faithful to her had been more fulfilling than any business deal could ever hope to be, and now Kate fully understood why Guy viewed his role in Villeneuve as a commitment for life.

And Megan was the sort of person who made a difference, Kate realised as she snuggled down under the covers. She had been a wonderful friend to Aunt Alice and now she was taking the Countess under her wing. After their emotional victory celebrations, Kate had wanted Guy's mother to stay another night, but when Guy had finally been forced to refuel and had rung them to say that he was on his way home the Countess had elected to return to the château—just to reassure herself that everything really was back to normal, she said, asking Megan to accompany her.

Villeneuve was her home too now, Kate realised as she waited for the familiar night sounds to lull her back to sleep. She would resign from the board of Freedom Holidays at the earliest opportunity and once she had managed to convince Guy that the guest house could only enhance his business plans for the estate, she would be free to concentrate all her energies on running Freedom Breaks at La Petite Maison.

# CHAPTER TEN

KATE shot bolt upright in bed as a shower of gravel skittered across her window followed by insistent knocking on the front door. Switching on the overhead lamp, she saw that it was just after two o'clock in the morning. Who called at this time, unless it was an emergency? she reasoned, swinging out of bed. Grabbing her robe, she ran down the stairs while any number of horrifying scenarios played out in her mind. Thanks to the lack of electricity she was forced to a halt just inside the kitchen and, fumbling in the dark, she managed to light a couple of candles before hurrying to the door.

Reminding herself that it could be anyone standing on the doorstep, she took a mental step back and yelled, 'Hello?'

'Kate, let me in.'

'Guy!' Fighting with the locks, she finally managed to get the door open and, gasping with relief, launched herself into his arms. 'Guy! I thought you were never coming back.'

'Try and keep me away,' he said huskily dragging her close.

'When did you get here?' she murmured, trailing fingertips across his stubble-roughened face. 'You look so tired,' she added, as she stared up at him with concern.

'I haven't wasted time sleeping,' he confirmed. 'But I really don't want to talk about my travel arrangements,' he added, eyes glinting with humour in the candlelight. And then he proved the point with a hard, hungry kiss.

He felt so warm and rough and strong. The rasp of his beard against her face as he kissed her was the most wonderful sensation on earth. Nothing came close to knowing that Guy wanted her. It set her senses alight. She gave herself up to him, moulding herself against him, not troubling to hide her hunger as she drew him with her into the house.

'Hey, hey,' Guy cautioned in a whisper as, capturing her chin in his hand, he looked into her eyes. 'What about Megan?'

'She's staying at the château,' Kate explained, 'With your mother. I'm here on my own.' She watched as his sensuous lips slowly curved into a smile.

'In that case, can you give me a bed for the night?'

She gave her answer with her hands, her lips and her eyes, and when they broke apart she said softly, 'Where have you been?' Then, meshing her fingers through his hair, she pulled him close as if to keep him with her for ever.

'Putting those damned covenants to bed once and for all,' he said, taking her hands in his so that he could kiss each fingertip in turn.

'How did you do that?'

'My legal team tracked down some original documents lodged in a vault in Paris,' Guy told her. 'Then they needed me to testify in court.'

'And?'

'The case closed successfully late yesterday and in our favour.'

'Oh, Guy, I'm so happy for you!' Kate said as she burrowed her face into his chest.

'Happy for us, *mon coeur*,' he corrected huskily, cupping her chin and bringing her face up. 'I rang the château. I heard what you did—for my mother and for Villeneuve. I can't believe you had to go through all that alone—'

'I'm not a little girl now, Guy. And I only did what had to be done—'

*'Mais magnifiquement!'*

'Now even I'm impressed,' she teased him gently as his admiration for her spilled over into his own language.

'Be serious for a moment, *chérie*,' he implored. 'How can I thank you when you're like this?'

Kate withheld her suggestion and said instead, 'So, you aren't angry with me any more?'

'Angry with you?' Guy murmured incredulously as he brushed away the sleep-tangled hair from her face. 'For goodness' sake, Kate, what are you talking about?'

Swallowing hard, Kate came straight out with it. 'My guest house, the fact that I pushed ahead with my plans without so much as consulting you and—'

'Sometimes it's good to have an input of new ideas,' he murmured, staring at her with an intensity that looped a band of love around her soul. 'Who says I have all the right answers?'

'As far as I'm concerned, you have most of them,' Kate breathed, her lips almost touching his.

'Only most of them?' he said in a voice not much above a whisper as he began teasing her lips with his tongue.

When he finally stopped kissing her for a moment, Guy shot a look around the blacked-out room and frowned as he weighed up the flickering candles. 'Why are you still in the dark?'

'Because the electricity's off again,' Kate said wryly, breaking away to find some more candles.

'*J'y crois pas!*' Guy exclaimed as he reached out to haul her back. 'Didn't I sort that out for you once already?'

He would believe it if he knew how vindictive Mariamme D'Arbo had been, Kate thought ruefully. But hadn't Ms D'Arbo done enough damage already? She would spare him the detail for now. 'You did sort it out,' she confirmed. 'This is just a glitch. I'll see about it tomorrow.' And when he tried to argue she put her fingers over his lips. 'Guy, I really don't want to talk about electricity.' She saw his expression change from indignation to amusement and then on again to something different.

'*Ma petite héroïne,*' he murmured wryly as he wrapped

his arms around her and nuzzled her neck. 'You have no idea how much I love you, do you?'

'You love me?' Kate whispered while she still could.

Dragging her close, he kissed the breath out of her while his hands roved freely over her trembling body, naked apart from the oversized tee shirt she wore to bed. Before she knew what was happening he had pulled it over her head. Then, gripping her just below the waist, he turned her slowly to face away from him. 'Now I see why you wanted these mirrors,' he said with a low, sexy laugh.

'Guy!' Kate protested without much force. She dragged in a long shuddering breath as she watched his hands move very slowly to claim her breasts. Then his lean, supple fingers started work on her nipples until they grew so erect she could only press back against him with her eyes fixed on the seductive reflection—which she knew was just what he intended. Without giving her a chance to ease down from the high erotic plateau, Guy hooked a padded bench with his foot and nudged against the back of her legs until she was kneeling on it. As he eased her over the counter Kate felt the chill of cold granite replace the warmth of his hands. Then a powerful thigh came to lodge between her legs as he looped one arm around her waist while he loosened his zipper and tugged off his beige chinos.

Every sensory zone seemed to be swelling on command and, as his touch grew more urgent Kate angled towards him, shamelessly craving more. In the otherwise silent room their breathing sounded hectic and, suddenly aware of it, she met his gaze in their reflected world. But Guy only granted her the briefest glance. He was already clasping her buttocks, ready to direct and control. Kate found the intensity of his concentration only heightened her arousal and, as he made a slow and deliberately tantalising pass, she thrust towards him, taking him by surprise as she captured him and drew him deep inside her. For a moment, lost in fierce pleasure, he remained completely still.

'Don't stop,' she managed to beg as his eyes flashed up a warning. 'I need you so much.'

Guy won the next round easily, with a withdrawal so slow Kate felt every nerve-ending go into spasm. But, just as she started whimpering with disappointment, he plunged deep again, increasing his grip as he brought her steadily into rhythm with him. He answered all her needs as he took her with him to the highest peak of pleasure, choosing the moment to step off into a shuddering cascade of sensation that left them both convulsing violently with an intensity that left them clinging to each other thoroughly shaken.

Minutes passed before either of them was even capable of speech and then Kate asked shyly, 'Did you mean it? Do you really love me?'

*'Tu es la personne à laquelle je tiens le plus au monde!'* Guy exclaimed. 'I'm sorry,' he said with a wry laugh as he gathered her up in his arms. 'What have you done to me, Kate? I couldn't even think in English for a moment. Of course I love you. How can you doubt it?'

'So you—'

'I just told you in French that you are the most special person to me in all the world.'

'And I love you…more than my life,' Kate breathed, knowing it was true.

'For all your life?' Guy murmured as he swung her off the ground.

'For all my life,' Kate confirmed softly as she nestled against him.

'Come, *mon coeur*,' Guy said, heading for the stairs. 'It's time for bed.'

The first cockerels were already heralding the gauzy light of a new day when they finally fell into a deep and contented slumber. The stress of the past few days and the fact that Guy had had little sleep had made no impression at all on their hunger for each other. It was as if no amount of lovemaking could ever be enough; as if they needed to make up for every single moment they had been apart.

And when Kate finally woke in Guy's arms, it was to find him drinking in every detail of her face as if they had only just met.

'Sometimes I can't believe this moment has come,' he murmured as he kissed her brow, her cheeks and, with lingering intensity, her lips.

'Why not?' Kate queried softly, linking her hands loosely behind his neck so that she could look into his face.

'Because I wanted you the moment you walked back into my life,' Guy admitted easily. 'But the age difference—'

'It's not so much,' Kate told him with a grin. 'Just enough to ensure you know what you're doing in the bedroom department...' She squealed with delight as he made a grab for her.

'You are still *incorrigible!*' he exclaimed, seeming pleased. 'But you must be serious for a moment—'

'If you insist.'

'I do insist,' he said, pretending to be stern as he let her soft golden hair stream through his fingers. 'I can't imagine now how I held off from seducing you for as long I did—'

'You're very confident,' Kate teased with all the assurance his love had given her.

'Completely confident,' he said, with brutally male assurance. 'I confess it took time for me to appreciate that you are not the same little Kate who used to visit her aunt in Villeneuve each year—'

'But I am the same person,' Kate warned teasingly.

'In some ways,' Guy admitted tolerantly. 'But you have matured into a very beautiful woman.'

'Well, improved at least, I hope,' Kate qualified. 'Like a good wine?'

'*Exactement,*' Guy agreed, his steely eyes twinkling with humour.

'So, now it's time to taste me?' she guessed provocatively.

'Let's just say I'm overwhelmed by you and by everything you do.'

'Does that mean you approve of my activities at the cottage?'

'You never miss an opportunity, do you *mon ange*?' Guy demanded in a voice laced with dry amusement. 'But I am forced to admit that it is the rebel in you that has always attracted me.'

'Taming the tiger?' Kate suggested innocently.

'Well, the pussy cat at least,' he said, knowing how that would provoke her.

Kate knew he took great pleasure in pinning her down when she made a lunge for him. 'And is that all you find attractive about me?' she demanded, making a pretence of being disappointed.

Guy let his gaze rove slowly over the length of her before commenting, 'There are one or two other attractions—'

'Brute!' she flared, trying to escape.

'Why don't you just learn to give in?' Guy suggested evenly as she continued to struggle ineffectually against his controlling hands.

'Never!'

'Well, you should calm down or you might miss what I have to say to you.'

Feigning a frown, Kate made a sound of begrudging capitulation and then finally lay still.

'That's better,' Guy told her.

'So?' Kate prompted. 'What do you have to say to me?'

'First, I'd like to thank you for giving my mother a new lease of life—'

'That was my pleasure and you know it,' she challenged. 'So that can't be what you have to say. What else is there?'

'Thank you for pointing out the fact that I should not rely on an agency to supply crucial members of my staff—'

'Mariamme D'Arbo?'

'Exactly,' he admitted. 'Did you know she stole Mother's ring?'

'The police have assured me they have recovered it,' Kate said. 'It was the first thing I checked on when Mariamme D'Arbo was arrested.'

'Let's move on to your plans to run a guest house on my estate—'

'You don't mind, after all?' Kate said hopefully, struggling to read Guy's unreadable expression.

'There is one condition—'

'And that is?'

'I insist that you base yourself at the château.'

'At the château?' Kate queried as she worked the idea through in her mind. 'It could work out,' she murmured. 'If your mother moved into the cottage—'

'Ah, I was hoping you'd say that,' Guy cut in with some satisfaction.

'Why?'

'Because she confided in me,' he revealed. 'She explained that the big house is too full of painful memories for her. Everywhere she turns she sees my father—'

'I can understand that,' Kate said, suddenly serious. 'They were together for so long, Guy. If I can do anything…anything at all to help—'

'I think you can,' he said, matching her mood. 'The warmth and camaraderie at La Petite Maison has had such a healing effect on her I don't want it to stop. She says she is happier now than she has been since the accident and that it is all due to your return and the wonderful atmosphere you have created at the cottage. And, with your agreement, Kate, I thought she might find contentment again, given time.'

'Of course she's welcome,' Kate said warmly. 'Your mother can have all the time she needs—and that's not just for her benefit, but for ours too. She's been the most wonderful help. Everyone loves her. And not just because she's the Countess—she's so full of ideas and so interesting to be around.'

'And she has gained so much from you and from Megan and from your guests.'

Kate felt it only fair to warn him. 'They may not all be as charming as the last group.'

'I think you'll find she has some steel in her backbone along with that old-world charm,' he said wryly. 'She's taking a real interest in life again, Kate. Something I thought I'd never see—'

'You really don't have to twist my arm,' Kate insisted. 'You know how much I love your mother, Guy. And if she could take charge of things here with Megan... Well, I could easily hold cookery classes at the château. The kitchen is more than adequate for my needs—'

'I am relieved to hear it,' he said solemnly. 'Here in Villeneuve we like to do things as a team.'

'Mmm,' Kate sounded in contemplation, her forehead puckering as she thought over his words. Then her face cleared as she came to a decision. 'You really don't know how lucky you are to belong to something as special as this.'

'Oh, but I do,' he said. 'Don't you, Kate?'

'Me? Guy, are you teasing me again?' Kate demanded, suddenly suspecting he might be. As he ran his hands lightly over her arms she began to tremble, certain now that he was only playing games with her as he always had.

He shook his head in fond exasperation. 'You're as much a part of Villeneuve as I am, Kate. Deep down you always knew that to be the case. That's why you came back.'

'You're very wise,' she said softly, snuggling into the pillows again as his gaze warmed her face.

'So—' Guy drawled with his unique brand of male satisfaction '—if I'm so wise, you won't think it foolish of me when I ask you to marry me.'

Kate's eyes widened as she turned a face blank with surprise in Guy's direction.

'I can't promise you an easy ride, at least not to begin

with,' he went on evenly. 'I still have some issues with the property that I've yet to resolve.'

A bolt of sensation thrilled through Kate as she went on staring at him.

'But from what I've seen so far—' he continued, clearly oblivious to the chaotic state of her emotions '—I think you can handle it.'

'Yes, Guy.'

'I have to tell you, your use of the DNA test was a really great—'

'Yes, Guy,' Kate said a little more insistently.

He stopped and looked down at her, his expressive grey eyes eloquent with enquiry.

'Yes, I will marry you,' Kate said steadily, gazing up with a heart full of love into the eyes of the man around whose roots she now understood she had always been entwined.

'Little Katie Foster…all grown up,' he murmured softly, tucking a wayward curl behind her ear.

'That's right,' Kate whispered as she gazed into his eyes. 'Grown up with you and for you, Guy.' Then her expression changed to one he knew of old. 'But are you quite sure you can put up with me?'

He pretended to think about it for a moment. 'I can only try. Do you think you can put up with being the Countess de Villeneuve?'

Kate's lips curved in wry acceptance as she lifted her shoulders in the pretence of a shrug. 'I can only try,' she said cheekily as he gathered her up in his arms and kissed her.

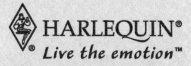

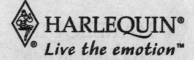

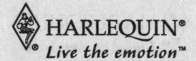

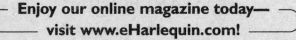

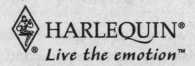

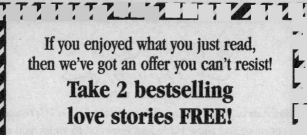

If you enjoyed what you just read,
then we've got an offer you can't resist!

# Take 2 bestselling love stories FREE!

# Plus get a FREE surprise gift!

---

**Clip this page and mail it to Harlequin Reader Service®**

| **IN U.S.A.** | **IN CANADA** |
|---|---|
| 3010 Walden Ave. | P.O. Box 609 |
| P.O. Box 1867 | Fort Erie, Ontario |
| Buffalo, N.Y. 14240-1867 | L2A 5X3 |

**YES!** Please send me 2 free Harlequin Presents® novels and my free surprise gift. After receiving them, if I don't wish to receive anymore, I can return the shipping statement marked cancel. If I don't cancel, I will receive 6 brand-new novels every month, before they're available in stores! In the U.S.A., bill me at the bargain price of $3.57 plus 25¢ shipping & handling per book and applicable sales tax, if any*. In Canada, bill me at the bargain price of $4.24 plus 25¢ shipping & handling per book and applicable taxes**. That's the complete price and a savings of at least 10% off the cover prices—what a great deal! I understand that accepting the 2 free books and gift places me under no obligation ever to buy any books. I can always return a shipment and cancel at any time. Even if I never buy another book from Harlequin, the 2 free books and gift are mine to keep forever.

106 HDN DNTZ
306 HDN DNT2

| Name | | (PLEASE PRINT) | |
|---|---|---|---|
| Address | | Apt.# | |
| City | State/Prov. | | Zip/Postal Code |

\* Terms and prices subject to change without notice. Sales tax applicable in N.Y.
\*\* Canadian residents will be charged applicable provincial taxes and GST.
   All orders subject to approval. Offer limited to one per household and not valid to
   current Harlequin Presents® subscribers.
   ® are registered trademarks of Harlequin Enterprises Limited.

PRES02                                      ©2001 Harlequin Enterprises Limited

The world's bestselling romance series.

## HARLEQUIN®
### *Presents*

**Seduction and Passion Guaranteed!**

*Your dream ticket to the vacation of a lifetime!*

Why not relax and allow Harlequin Presents® to whisk you away
to stunning international locations with our new miniseries...

*Where irresistible men and sophisticated women
surrender to seduction under the golden sun.*

Don't miss this opportunity to
experience glamorous lifestyles
and exotic settings in:

**Robyn Donald's
THE TEMPTRESS OF TARIKA BAY**
on sale July, #2336

**THE FRENCH COUNT'S MISTRESS**
by Susan Stephens
on sale August, #2342

**THE SPANIARD'S WOMAN**
by Diana Hamilton
on sale September, #2346

**THE ITALIAN MARRIAGE**
by Kathryn Ross
on sale October, #2353

*FOREIGN AFFAIRS... A world full of passion!*

**Pick up a Harlequin Presents® novel and you will enter a world
of spine-tingling passion and provocative, tantalizing romance!**

*Available wherever Harlequin books are sold.*

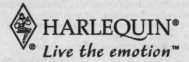

## HARLEQUIN®
### *Live the emotion*™

**Visit us at www.eHarlequin.com**

HPFAMA